Coachella

Coachella

Sheila Ortiz Taylor

University of New Mexico Press

Albuquerque

Library of Congress Cataloging-in-Publication Data

Taylor, Sheila Ortiz, 1939–

Coachella / Sheila Ortiz Taylor—1st ed.

p. cm.

ISBN 0-8263-1843-6

1. Mexican Americans—California—Coachella Valley—Fiction.

2. AIDS (Disease)—Patients—California—Coachella Valley—Fiction.

3. Mexican American lesbians—California—Coachella Valley—Fiction.

I. Title

PS3570. A9544C63 1998

813'. 54—DC21   97–34080

CIP

Designed by Sue Niewiarowski

For Joy

Acknowledgments

✐ I wrote this book amidst wise and kind people in landscapes that challenged and inspired my imagination, thanks to residencies granted by the Cottages at Hedgebrook (1995, Langley, Washington) and La Fundación Valparaíso (1996, Almería, Spain).

Special thanks to Andrea Otañez, Therese Stanton, and Joy Lynn Lewis for reading and rereading the manuscript; to Juan Bruce-Novoa, Monifa Love, and Lisa Glatt for talking art with me; to Anne Rowe for her confidence and support; and to Laura Taff for her help with Crescencio's history.

I am grateful to Florida State University for travel grants that helped underwrite my research expenses.

Excerpts from this novel have appeared in *Review of Contemporary Fiction, Apalachee Quarterly, Americas Review,* and *Proceedings of the Seventh International Conference on Latino Cultures in the United States.*

*Until the end of 1984, blood bank authorities sought
to interpret observations on post transfusion AIDS
as minor accidents and refused to draw appropriate
practical inferences from it. . . . The CDC moved with
a great deal of consideration for the institutions under
question. A screening program was put in place only in
March 1985. Thus for eight years a path of infection
remained mostly open for the AIDS virus . . .*
—Mirko D. Grmek
History of AIDS: Emergence and Origin of a Modern Pandemic

*In the Coachella Valley, the DAP estimates one in
every 20 persons living here may already have
contracted the HIV virus.*
—Palm Springs *Desert Sun*, 1995

Book One

1 ✐ Crescencio Ramírez is kneeling in the petunias by the patio when he hears the water begin its rush into the side bed. Makes him feel the need to relieve himself, to tell the truth. All that water pouring out onto sand. And by the clock, like everything gringo. It's time, it's time, they always say.

But this lady is different, his lady. La señora. He can just make out the foot of her bed behind the heavy gold curtain pulled open against the sliding door. For her he plants these petunias, double ones, here, where she can maybe see them from her rented hospital bed. Petunias, her most favorite flower.

He resettles his straw hat on his thick gray curls and slices with his knife through the flat of young plants, taking out another, examining the white threadlike tendrils, and nestling it into a hole. He presses the earth around the roots, edges forward on his knees, starts a new hole.

Yesterday ese hombre, her husband, this Mr. Townsend, had come outside—in his pajamas—to say that if he, Crescencio, dug all his holes at once, entonces, if he put peat moss in all of them, and having done all this, then he put the plants in, all at once, that he would save time.

Gringo time otra vez. Like time could be put in a bank. Depósito. Like you could take it out when you needed some.

Think of Henry Ford, this man kept telling him, hair sticking out all over his head like some crazy palm tree, the sun behind him, making Crescencio squint as he looked up, always looking up at the man over him. The man telling him to think of Henry Ford.

Well, Crescencio has a Ford truck himself, and is an American now same as Mr. Townsend. He knows a thing or two. He knows if he did his planting de esa manera—assembly line—there would be no pleasure. And then the plants would not care to put down their roots or to stretch toward the sun. No. Each thing done carefully and in its own time.

He places both palms down on the warming soil, easing the weight from his knees.

Claro you could make money that other way—Crescencio knows this—and buy big houses, cars with phones and TVs in them, and pay other people to drive you around, fix your dinner, wash your clothes, mow your grass. Then make them feel stupid, like they don't know their own job.

He cuts out another plant, loosens the roots so they will spread.

His lady should have a man worthy of her and worthy of the name. Un verdadero hombre. Somebody to look out for her. Take care of her.

They said that she herself was a Mexican lady. Oh, you

couldn't see it so much by her skin; una güera. It was the way she turned her head and looked at you. It was in the manner of her listening. La sangre.

He hears the water begin flowing around the bottlebrush now and the oleander. Around the grapefruit and the oranges. The roses and the bougainvillea. Water brought from a long way off or pumped out of the rivers running under the streets of the city, they say, water to keep this place not looking like a desert at all. Everything green.

Sure, he has a little garden himself, back at his place in Horse Thief Canyon, grows some corn, squash, carrots, tomatoes, peppers, onions. Cilantro, sage, parsley. Nada más. Just for his familia. The rest of his yard is mostly sand and cactus and snakes. Gary Luna's old black Chevy pickup falling to pieces.

But you couldn't call the desert dead. Tourists did, with their talk. He heard them in the drugstore where they came smelling of chlorine and coconut oil, their eyes lost behind dark glasses. But if you let her, la yerma, she had a way almost of making love to you. Surprises. Always some kind of flower coming out of those cactuses: yellow, pink, red. And in the winter, the palo verde made her blossoms of amarillo and the canyon filled with bright wildflowers. Just for a while, then gone. But always the sweet smell of the desert willow near his window. Chuparosa blossoms brought the hummingbirds.

All these plants took care of themselves. God must be their gardener. He laughs. Here, *he* is God. Creating petunias. He presses another into the ground. For la señora. Mops his brow, holds his bandanna over the sprinkler to wet it good, puts the damp cloth on his head underneath his hat. The day's heating up. He looks at the shadows to give him the time, remembering.

6

Remembering her before her infirmities. Remembering their meeting. A candy striper lady at the hospital, she was. She had come to his wife's room every day bringing magazines, jugs of fresh water, reading stories out of *Reader's Digest* to cheer her up, inspire her. For weeks. Until finally La Virgen took his dear one away. The cancer growing inside her like some kind of crazy thorned plant.

And she had come, la señora, had come to the rosary at night and the funeral next day. Had touched his daughter on the arm. Had sent flowers. Was herself a blossom growing in the crevices of his grief.

And now she too is sick. Where have all these enfermedades come from, he wants to know?

He settles the velvet petunia into the soil, presses it firmly, shapes a little impression around it to hold moisture against the hardships of the desert. The sun so hot. He leans back, straightening his spine, feeling those two hurting places lining up and easing down. Bueno.

His nephew Jaime's always telling him he should go to work for the golf courses, quit working for eight, ten, twelve different people, some of them paying real regular, like la señora, others not. Too busy saving time to pay him. Get some benefits, Tío, Jaimito would tell him.

He sprinkles peat moss into the next hole.

That's fine for Jaime. Gary Luna's boy. Riding around on green machines big as dinosaurs, spraying poisons, fertilizer, being—¿cómo se dice?—un fairway management specialist. Well, he, Crescencio Ramírez, is just a gardener, as God has made him.

An old man, seguro, but able to work. He's okay, has his health. Crescencio crosses himself lightly over his brown work shirt. His daughter has a good job. With benefits. But no husband. If he just knew for sure she had somebody to take care of her, look out for her, that's all. Like if something was to happen to him.

That's what it came down to, didn't it? ¿Siempre?

He looks again at the foot of la señora's bed. This life was hard and yet things seemed to be getting worse, felt like to him. Had it always been like this? People getting robbed, hit over the head, shot, dumped in dry washes. They found them every day, but especially after the flash floods. You could read about it in the newspaper. Dead bodies all over the desert, like trash. Nobody knew how they got there and nobody cared.

This air getting bad, too, with the smog. He glances toward the Santa Rosas, studies the thin yellow layer—like a bruise—just beyond the freeway. People getting sick from it. People getting sick and nobody knowing why. Just from breathing, seemed like.

And those doctors. He has no use for them. He slices through the next row of petunias, feeling the wooden handle of the knife against the ridges of his palm.

Seems like they would have been able to help this lady. Know what was wrong with her at least. Give her something to call it so she wouldn't feel plain loca.

All this trouble—he thinks—really started with them. Esos doctores. Had started with that operation she had two, maybe three years ago. ¿Cómo se dice? The liposuction, that's it. His daughter, Yolanda, who works at the hospital y por eso knows of such things, said it was like running a vacuum cleaner around inside a woman, taking off flesh that was alive, healthy. Like it wasn't natural or right to carry weight in that womanly way.

So they ran that vacuum all around inside her, and she bled so much she had to have blood, was in bad pain for weeks. Moved so slow you could almost feel the hurt. And all for nothing. Then she got flu right after, entonces the pneumonia. She had never been right since. This and that. Somebody who had been kind toda su vida, you knew just by looking at her.

La señora. Eliana. He speaks her name softly inside his head so the sound of it is like the wind caressing the date palms. He rocks back on his heels, gazes at fingers of sunlight moving softly up into the wrinkles of the mountain, listens to the voices of the mourning doves. Then, standing slowly—the last petunia planted—he breathes in the heavy scent of orange, the murmur of bees, the movement of water.

2 ✑ Pigeon stands under Desert Hot Springs' winter sun, dwarfed by landscape and grief. The pastor's voice

drones through the chill and breezy morning in a monotonous litany of consolation, but Pigeon is not listening to his empty words. Pain seeps into her cells like boiling hot water—agua caliente—like the mineral springs she used to steep in twice a week at the Palm Springs Spa, in happier times.

Now she is alone in a lifeless desert. Though she stands under the shuddering canvas marquee with her friends, her brother Brice, she feels all these people surrounding her suddenly as heavy pieces of rock. Like the Easter Island stone figures she once saw in a doctor's office copy of *National Geographic*.

Inside that casket her sleeping Edward is more alive than these people had ever been, more alive than she herself would ever be. Pigeon stifles a sudden intake of breath that rises dangerously toward a sob. Edward could never bear to see her cry, would lean his face in close for consolation, to share her suffering.

How many of these people here are truly sharing her pain, how many have ever known true intimacy? She sees now the paucity of their lives, feels her own life swerve in the direction of trivia and sterility, following the path already cleared for her by these walking dead.

The pastor has finished, places a red rose on the handsomely carved coffin lid, murmurs a blessing, then approaches Pigeon, his hands held out in a gesture of invitation and consolation.

Suddenly out of the group lunges Tootie Greenwald, almost knocking him aside, mascara streaked in startling little rivulets down her looming face. "Pigeon," she is saying, much too close, her perfume overpowering the surrounding air, "trust me dear, you must replace him just as soon as you possibly can."

Pigeon stumbles back, holds up her hand as if to ward off a semi-truck bearing down. Then her brother steps in, takes charge, guides Tootie away, his hand under her elbow as he murmurs in low tones about friendship and the need to be strong for one another.

Pigeon looks up high into snow-covered Mount San Jacinto, the cold immensity of it, monolithic, jagged as her own mourning heart. The pastor takes her hands, looks into her drowning eyes, tells her she must somehow go on, must think of her work, her vital work for the hospital. She must stay the course for Edward, go on in his name.

When her chest again falls into regular rhythms of breathing, the pastor lets go one hand and gives an invisible sign to the director from Mountain View Memorial Park, who has been waiting, frozen in the rituals of death. Now the director kneels down on a piece of purple satin, leans forward with the coffin in his right hand, and gently sets it into the ground.

As if by design, automated sprinklers rise in the golf course beyond the sculpture garden and the hedge. Shhik, shhik, shhik, Colorado River water sketching helixes across desert sky.

3 ✐ A woman stands in the doorway of her trailer, barefoot, gazing out at patterned light and shadow

falling on the Indio Hills and the mountains beyond. The morning sun illuminates her hair, a mane so thick and dark that in this light it turns a deep plum. Her baby sleeps under a blanket on the double bed in the next room, guarded by a chair, two stacked suitcases.

The woman stands in the doorway, sensing with her bare feet the uneven texture of the cheap checkerboard linoleum, worn, buckled, and ripped slightly under the strain of so many exits and entrances, people whose journeys continue somewhere else.

She takes the sun of this winter morning on her face, holds a cup of coffee, breathes in the desert stillness, unaware of the man planting flowers in Palm Springs, the woman burying her dog in Desert Hot Springs.

She is not thinking about where she has come from or what will happen next. She simply stands in the doorway of this rented trailer in Coachella, feeling in her hand both the coffee cup and the mountain.

4 ✑ Biscuit Reed, volunteer at the Coachella Public Library on Tuesdays and Thursdays, and at Angel View Thrift Shop in Palm Springs on Mondays and Wednesdays (taking only Fridays for herself, unless Harold needs her to help out at the hospital), is worried about that attractive young Mexican woman with the thick black hair who has come in twice that she knows of to read obituaries out of old newspapers.

It just doesn't seem healthy to dwell on death like that,

let alone somebody so young, their whole life ahead of them. Biscuit has read enough magazines to know that death is perfectly natural. But isn't life natural too?

Biscuit brings the stamp down firmly on the form pasted into the flyleaf of a book: FEBRUARY 15 1983. Biscuit likes it in the library where everything is so neat and quiet. Likes it whenever Sally Augustino is busy in the back and she can kind of pretend—just to herself—that she, Biscuit Reed, is the librarian. She likes pressing the return date on all the books with the stamp, a way of expressing her belief that everything eventually would find its way back home again. The books and pamphlets would return, directed by the call numbers carefully stenciled on the spines, the codes identifying exactly where on the shelf they belonged.

A shaft of sun makes its way past the date palm guarding the east window and lights up the young woman's hair so that to Biscuit it almost looks purple. Must be natural, though, because nobody in their right mind would color their hair like that on purpose. Pretty though, like the way light hits a bowl of plums on the kitchen table in the morning.

Biscuit must have let herself look too intensely, though, because the woman in the purple hair squirms a little the way people sometimes do even when you're careful (having only glanced at them behind you in the mirror of your compact or sideways in a shop window), and she gets right up from the microfiche machine—her chair making a little backwards screek—to find more obituaries.

And so slim, this young woman. Biscuit can remember a

time when she herself weighed only ninety-eight pounds and had a little bitsy waist. Harold would laugh when his two big hands fit clear around. Last summer she'd decided to go ahead and have that tummy tuck after all. Otherwise she just knew they would not have asked her to model ever again in the Springtime Fatimas of the Fez Hospital Benefit Fashion Show. She would have joined the lonely ranks of those who had let themselves go.

But she hadn't realized something called a tummy tuck could hurt so much or take so long to get over. And her belly button had come out in a different place, off to one side. Dr. Glass had said that was not unusual and he didn't guess she'd be wearing a bikini anyway. With clothes on, it was true, her stomach looked flat again, especially when she wore control-top panty hose. She was glad, all in all, that she'd had that tummy tuck when she did and that the work of it was behind her now.

But only that morning she had got a real shock. When she finished reading Ann Landers in the "Living" section of the *Desert Sun* and her eye wandered down the page, she saw an ad with the challenging question: "Is it time for facial rejuvenation?"

Time, she had thought. All her life being a woman had meant it was time for something: time to get breasts, time to get your period, time to go steady, get engaged, get married, time to have babies, get on the pill, go through the change, stop her stomach from pooching. And now maybe it was time to start in on her face. Rejuvenate it.

She stamps FEBRUARY 15 1983 upside down on the next book. Then the door swings open and Biscuit glances up. It's that man who wears lipstick. Well it *is* lipstick but very light. Almost tasteful. Biscuit herself is broad-minded, but it's harder for Harold because men naturally feel insecure about their manhood.

She had seen an in-depth program about this very topic on "Good Morning, America" one morning when she was getting over her tummy tuck. So she knew tolerance was not something she could ever expect to learn from Harold. No, it was really her friend Eliana Townsend who had shown her about accepting gay people for whatever they happened to be at the moment.

It was at a party at the Townsends', before Ellie got so sick. Christmas, it had been. And everything very fancy but tasteful in that beautiful Spanish house of theirs right on the golf course, Shadow Hills, that's where. Well, there was to be live entertainment. Nobody knew what. Something very special. So everybody was excited, waiting. Finally, out comes this gorgeous show girl, slinks up to the baby grand and leans on it, batting her eyelashes.

It was Leonard! Leonard Lowe the architect. Always so manly and quiet and conservative. But that night he was Lowella, with the most gorgeous legs you've ever seen and a voice to match. Honestly, you would never have dreamed it was a man at all.

Well Harold was fit to be tied, but too much of a professional ever to say anything in public, of course. This other man, though—with that exclusive new development, Rancho del Sol Estates in Cathedral City?—said right out loud that people like that just made him sick to his stomach.

Ellie, she just drew herself up—they say she comes from Spanish nobility—and she told him to go home. Just like that. Like he was a little boy. Go on home now. And he left. You should have seen the look on his face.

The man in the lipstick sitting on the couch reading the *Wall Street Journal* fingers his perm. He's wearing a teal green turtleneck sweater with a thick gold chain, winter white linen slacks, and white patent leather shoes to match. Everybody said they have lots of money, but it was hard to think anybody'd ever hire a man who permed his hair and wore lipstick. Even tasteful lipstick.

Biscuit stamps the date on the last of the books for the hospital and decides to start in on the overdue notices, because later on in the day—you could bet on it—things would really start to get out of hand.

5 ✐ The woman reading the Arizona obituaries in the Coachella Public Library keeps getting drawn into stories of the dead. She knows more about these people than she has ever known about the friends she left in Des Moines, the ones who—along with her husband—do not know where she is.

She knows names and ages, the relationships and occupations of their survivors, sometimes what they died of, their faces floating into her imagination like drowned bodies rising.

She rests her pencil now beside one of the dead:

*Marina Luisa Lomas, born in Salton Sea Beach in 1957,
moved to Tucson, Arizona, in 1971.*

16   She sees Marina now, floating high on a sea of salt, surrounded by shimmering sea creatures, half women, half fish:
iridescent, opalescent. She hears Marina's husband hailing
her from shore, her aged parents imploring her to return to
Tucson, to life. But she is borne on by the haunting songs of
these mermaids, the flap of their scaled tails in purpling water.
Breasting the current, she heads for the open sea.

This woman in the library before whom shimmering histories rise up is looking for a name. Something easily exchanged,
replaced. Someone to become. Someone to change herself
into. Searching back through Arizona months, she has been
seeking a corpse willing to strike a bargain: her own iden-
tity for theirs. Gathering her past about her like a blue cloak,
she invokes sacred and powerful names. Coatlicue, she murmurs, Malintzin, Tonantzin, Guadalupe.

*

That night, by the time she sits in her kitchen at her green
formica table, Isabel Ochoa Dryfus has already turned into
Marina Lomas. Simply Marina Lomas of Tucson, Arizona.
Someone with no history.

Under her kitchen's flickering fluorescent light she carefully writes by hand the first letter, the one to Social Secu-

rity asking for a replacement card. A replacement for the one she has lost. Whose number she does not even remember. From that one letter, all else will eventually follow: a new driver's license, voter registration, food stamps, maybe even a credit card. She has learned how to do this from reading the mystery novels David brought her when she was a girl in Mexico.

17

Tonight, in a trailer in Coachella—under desert stars and quarter moon—a woman is writing the letter that will begin everything. This Marina Lomas of Tucson, Arizona.

1 ⌟ It's about nine in the morning when Marina Lomas arrives at the Casa Diva Guest House. She sees a tall, slender man with red hair standing at the end of the pool, brushing downward in slow swoops. She is not sure if he is the pool man or the person she spoke to on the phone, the owner.

Light strikes jagged bars deep through the volumed water, shimmers over the surface, paints a fluid range of blues that remind her of the colors in her father's tile factory in Juárez; the colors in her paintings at the school of design in San Luis; the self from which she has crawled away. Colors play in her eyes until she can't see the man anymore.

Then he is coming her way, water dripping off the long brush, his feet flapping in plastic thongs. And she sees that he is much older than she had thought, maybe forty-five; his skin like parchment, his hair perhaps dyed, neatly cut, close to his head. In his striped shirt his shoulders slope downward as if he has somehow been permanently melted by desert heat.

"Marina?" he says, setting down the long pole and extending his hand. "Ah, good. Welcome to Casa Diva. I'm Bob. Bob

McVay. People call me Mac." There is an odd disjuncture between his melted features and his lively talk. He motions her into a white plastic chair under a pink and green striped umbrella.

They are alone on the patio, surrounded by empty lounge chairs in postures of exhaustion. All that white plastic looks to Marina like bones, as if she has somehow wandered into an elephant burial ground. White, she remembers, is the presence of all colors. Whatever is absent is also present.

He offers her coffee. Then Perrier. Marina shakes her head both times, looks around. "It's very quiet here."

"The boys are getting their beauty sleep. Late to bed and late to rise, I'm afraid."

"Boys?"

He pauses, looking at her. "Men. Gay men. This is a guest house for gay men." He looks briefly apologetic, then almost defiant. Lights a cigarette. Offers her one. She tells him she does not smoke.

"I shouldn't either," he smiles. Looks away, then suddenly back. Opens his mouth.

"Mr. McVay . . ."

"Mac," he corrects. "Just Mac."

"I need this job. I want to work for you. I have a daughter . . . a baby. Less than six months old. We've come here alone."

He is looking off toward the mountain, smoking. "This is the deal, then," he says, pauses, begins again. "This is the deal, Marina. My lover and I live back there." He nods in the direction of a two-story Mediterranean structure at the far end of the patio. "I need you to be a housekeeper for the guest house, make up the rooms, change the linen, that kind of thing, but I also need to know you'll help me out when Gil's not doing well."

20

"I don't understand."

"Gil's my partner, my family, really. Mostly he's fine, but now and again he comes down with this respiratory thing. In fact, let me get him for you. You can meet each other."

She puts out her arm, touches him lightly. "Don't bother him," she says. "It doesn't matter. I need this job. I'll do whatever I can."

"Sometimes he just needs somebody to be there, somebody to talk to." He smiles. "Well, more like somebody to listen to him. He holds his own in a conversation, I can tell you. And I love being audience for him, but there's the place to run."

It seems as if he will say more. She waits. The pool skimmer glugs. The odor of chlorine mixes with something sweet. Oranges maybe. Everywhere she looks, red plastic hummingbird feeders sway from branches in the morning breeze, columns of red liquid being drawn down by invisible birds.

"Sixteen units," he says, as if in answer to a thought she almost had. "A lot of work." He gets to his feet, remembering the work, as if it has grown in volume during their talk. "So what do you think, Marina? Deal?"

"You said minimum wage, but with a raise in three months."

"Let's say a raise in two, if everybody's happy." After they shake, he picks up a blue plastic box from the table. "I guess that about does it. Unless you've got questions."

"When do I start?" She fishes in her purse for her keys.

"Tomorrow morning? Oh, and just for the record, are you legal?"

"Yes and no," she says, not looking up, searching.

He laughs for the first time. "Yes and no. Well, that's a good one, Marina. That pretty much describes the rest of us. We're an alternative reality here at the Casa Diva. You'll feel very much at home.

"Now if you only knew something about test kits I'd be sure I had died and gone to heaven." He opens up the blue box, as if she will help.

She shakes her head, stands up, gathering her belongings. "No, but I *will* see you tomorrow morning."

"About eight thirty?" he says, taking out the connected plastic vials, stooping down, and running them through the pool water, then holding the contraption up to the light, a liquid Pan's pipe. "You know, once I didn't put in enough acid and by morning the whole pool turned red. The hummingbirds were ecstatic." He squeezes a dropper of yellow liquid into one of the vials and measures it against a chart in the lid, then holds it up to the light. "It's reading a very clear yes and no, Marina."

She smiles and heads for the car, jingling her keys.

2 ⌀ Yolanda Ramírez holds the vial up to the window. Damn, she's good at this. She can tell just by look-

ing that the white blood count is low. She knows it. But she puts it into the quaker and shaker machine, follows procedure, will in time write down the exact numbers. For the doctors to read soon as they get in from the golf course.

She takes out her lunch and eats it irreverently over the slides and the microscopes and the cultures. Sometimes she heats soup on the Bunsen burner. Today she has carrots and zucchini and tomatoes from her father's garden rolled up in a flour tortilla.

She thinks of Crescencio driving his battered old Ford pickup around the fancy developments, rakes sticking up, green hoses streaming behind. White Cadillacs and Town Cars veering around him thinking he has no insurance. Yolanda makes sure he has it, and that he remembers to pay the electricity, gas, phone. Since her mother died he forgets a lot. Or maybe he's just thinking about other things, other times. His lost Mexico. His lost world.

Well, Yo does what she can, but she has her own life to live. And he knows that. (She turns off the centrifuge, wipes her mouth on a paper towel, and takes the lid off the first vial.) When she told her mother in high school she was a lesbian, her mother had cried and said no no no mi'ja, you're not, you'll get over it.

Yo had quit school, moved out, worked at McDonald's, lived in an old Airstream, studied for her GED, then went nights to College of the Desert so she could get a decent job. This job. Phlebotomist One.

Her mother had never told her, Okay I was wrong. Never

said, You done good with your life, got an education, a car, your own home. Finally her mother had died mad in her heart at Yo and her ways. And now her father always asking when was she going to settle down, get married, raise a family. Refusing to admit, to know about her life, who she was, to see.

She places a smear of blood on a slide and fits it under the microscope's eye. Ah, what she likes is this world, the one that quivers in a drop, everything negotiating, nudging, embracing, oozing into, splitting off from everything else. She could stare forever.

Her supervisor, Silvia Cedeño, says curiosity killed the cat. Yo tells her time would tell.

Curiosity was being smart. Otherwise you were dead in the water. Little people, the ones pushed back, not seen, the silenced—those were the people who needed to stay curious no matter what it cost them. To ask the questions, the questions inside themselves, to keep on asking them. How come, how come, how come?

Why, Silvia had said, not noticing she was proving Yo's point. What was the good of asking, when nobody wanted to hear it, had their own problems? Get a life.

Go ahead, annoy everybody, Yo had said. Make me happy. If little people could stay curious long enough maybe they'd make big discoveries.

Like what? Silvia had wanted to know.

Por ejemplo. Por ejemplo a woman in her physics class at College of the Desert her last semester had told her about the Hudman belts of radiation. Yo had told her, You mean the Van Allen belts of radiation. No, the woman had said. She had been a clerk-typist for that famous physicist, James A. Van Allen. She said it was Anabelle Hudman, working in an office with no windows for peanuts who kept saying, What are all these high concentrations of energy about? Why do they form bands around the earth? So it was really Anabelle Hudman who discovered the Van Allen belts of radiation— not because she had a penis or a Ph.D. but because she was just plain curious, always kept looking for shapes, patterns, for whatever happened more than once. How come, how come, how come?

Silvia said, "But look who got the credit."

"Who the hell cares about the credit?" The beauty was in the finding. It didn't even matter if you were the first. Discovery was discovery.

Once she had bought a map of fault lines in the Coachella because somebody told her that her trailer was right on top of one. She spread that map out on the kitchen table, and something about the shape looked familiar. She got out her valley street map, put it under the topographical map, held the whole thing up against the bright kitchen window, and there it was. The dozen or so towns in the valley—from Desert Hot Springs on the west all the way to Thermal on the east— strung right along that San Andreas fault like goddamn jewels on a necklace.

Two weeks later she went hiking into Palm Canyon and found out why, what made this shape. She read it right there on the plaque outside the Indian gift shop. Anytime there was green space in the desert it was because the fault had buckled up and let water seep or rush up to the surface from underground rivers. Then she had followed the trail down into the canyon and stood there in the shade under giant shaggy palms, hundreds of years old—stood right where the Cahuillas had danced and mourned and loved and slept— and she felt the truth of it. An oasis was made out of something pushing its way past obstacles, seeking easy movement, freedom maybe. Oasis. She liked that word.

But oasis was just the top of something hidden underground—effect, not cause. And Yo had wanted to see straight into cause, root, el fondo, ground zero. Nothing less would satisfy. The book said Pushawalla Canyon for a straight shot, the real thing. So next week she was off to Pushawalla, where she had hooked her boot tips into solid rock and hung headfirst down over the fault itself, looking with her binoculars straight into it: el corazón. Alive, pulsing almost, with fierce stress. San Andreas.

So this was what she liked, all this, and she was glad to live on a fault and glad to be the one today handling this slide, covering it with glass, and reaching for the next vial, working with speed and style out of her own damn competence and curiosity.

3 ⌀ George Townsend stands in the bedroom doorway watching his wife sleep. They've been up half the night, and he has worked all morning to get her comfort-

able, and now finally she sleeps. He feels his own body relax, then slip down into exhaustion. He hasn't showered or shaved. Still in his pajamas, his thick green terry-cloth robe wrapped around him, he moves on dense carpeting down the hall and across the living room.

Out on the patio a breeze from the fairway stirs the palms. He phones the office to tell them he'll be late, again. Cold these winter days. He sinks back into the deep cushion of a patio chair, considers getting the morning paper, is too tired. Nothing ever in it anyway, except murder and mayhem. World going to hell in a handbasket, truth to tell. He puts his feet up on the ottoman, pulls his robe up tight around his neck.

Still, it's no good to think this way. Look on the bright side, Ellie always tells him. Each day is a miracle. Certainly he has come a long way in his own lifetime. He can see in his fatigue, in the strong thoughts about the power of women, a little scene in his head, like a magic lantern image, a picture from his boyhood: he and his mother seated at night in a glowing kitchen, she holding his outstretched hand, studying his palm, reading there that his father would throw him out of the house, that he would get a job as a candy boy on the Canadian railway, sleep at night in the rocking, clattering caboose, that he would join the army, fall in love with a beautiful woman, buy a business, raise daughters, learn to live in this world as a member of an up-and-coming community filled with health and enterprise.

No, where is the story taking him? What had his mother

really seen? What his mother must have read in his palm that night stopped with his father throwing him out of the house at thirteen. Only that could have been in the tableau. The rest he had made up himself.

But there was no shame in that. If he moved through life like a train through the night it was because he was strong in his wanting, in his believing in the shaping of a life out of nothing, a belief so strong and palpable it could sustain others. He had made himself up out of nothing, but he had not done it out of selfishness.

He is not his father. No, George Townsend is a man who—if need be—could hold others up, buoy them up in the flood, sustain them when their own weak efforts failed them. He sells insurance, after all, stands sentinel between his clients and impending disaster.

He gazes across the fairway. His life has been a kind of miracle, truth to tell. Here he is, a homeless boy, living on a golf course. And at the very moment that he sees this homeless Canadian boy standing, cap in hand, water springs up over on the ninth hole as if touched by a witching stick, something it does every day at this time, exactly at eleven A.M. So faithful you could set your watch by it. The spirit, the knowhow that created this oasis out of barren desert, a life out of nothing. This modern miracle.

His own sprinklers have turned themselves off. Crescencio always says it's a crime to water after ten in the morning because it fries the plants. Sun magnifies the drops. Says he'd rather come every day and water by hand because he doesn't like the timing devices, says he knows more about water and plants than any machine, any day. Always wanting to do things the hard way, that man. Dig each damn hole one at a time, put each plant in, one at a time. And you couldn't tell him anything. No, he'd just look at you in that way of his.

Ellie says Crescencio is always polite. And he is. Still, George sometimes feels judged by his own yardman. A man who would rather edge the damn grass with a machete while a perfectly good weed whacker stands in the garage collecting dust.

Never get anywhere that way. Not that George was prejudiced. No, he has known some very smart Mexicans in his time, but most of them—truth to tell—did things in this same half-assed way, everything one at a time.

He had thought more than once about letting Crescencio go. Shadow Hills handled all outdoor maintenance anyway. It was already paid for in their monthly fees. But his wife never liked the way maintenance did things, said they left ridges of grass standing, ran their mowers into the trunks of her trees. Besides, she always liked to do light gardening herself close up to the house, around the patio. Hanging pots. Flowers in planters. That kind of thing. Now Crescencio has taken over, until she gets better.

He notices for the first time flowers newly planted in the pots on the patio. Purple curly kind, like crushed Kleenexes. The wife loved them.

He listens for her now, half rises, sinks back down. Maybe he should hire a girl. Ellie had always preferred doing her own housework, and now all of it has fallen to him. Here he is running the Hoover over the carpet, making the beds, grocery shopping at night, giving Ellie her medicine, helping her bathe, racing off to the office, things there in an uproar, things here in an uproar.

He really can not take much more. He feels a sob rising to the surface like a drowning mole. A blind, wet thing.

He'll allow nothing pitiable about himself. Be sensible, he counsels. Ask Crescencio if he knows somebody, a girl to help out. Just for a while. Till Ellie can get on her feet.

He looks at the snow-covered mountain. Almost three years of sickness, off and on. Sometimes fine, sometimes not. Doctors said it was this then that, not knowing a damned thing. Then the one saying it was all in her head. Like to broke her spirit, telling her a thing like that! Made him mad as hell. So mad he feels it now, adrenalin flashing all through him, like a man struck by lightning.

He sees now in the red darkness behind his eyes his father rearing back to hit his mother hard across the mouth. Sees his own boy self leaping out wild and enraged, clinging helplessly for a moment to his father's back, trying to ride the fury, fingers ripping through the shirt, slipping, struggling for a purchase at his belt, then flung aside, skidding across the kitchen linoleum and into the legs of the pie safe, a useless heap.

Useless to her whom he had loved.

Somehow he had gone outside the magic lantern and pulled up another image, the one better forgotten. Sweat breaks out on his head, his chest. This is no way to think. He needs Ellie always telling him to look on the bright side, seeks out her voice inside himself.

He will feel better after his shower. He will feel better at work. He gets to his feet, placing two fingers on the table to steady himself. Tightening the sash of his robe, he moves deliberately toward the sliding door. It rolls back at his touch, admitting him into this sanctuary, his home. He is not the train boy.

February 26, 1983

    Yolanda stands in the shade of the palo verde,
adjusting the spray on the hose; then she strafes it over her
red Camaro, drops of water drumming flamenco on the hood.
It's Sunday, and she's feeling lazy, like it's a perfect day to
hang around here at home and avoid the crowds at the Date
Festival over in Indio. Later on she'll probably go over to her
father's for dinner, have some tamales with him and Tía Josie.
There's a volleyball game but she's not going to go. Last night
she stayed out late, shooting a little pool and dancing at Sister Jean's. She wrings the chamois out hard and walks around
soaping the roof, her wet sneakers crunching on the gravel
drive next to her Airstream.

    Yo bought this trailer for a song from a guy who lost his
shirt at the new Bingo Palace the Indians started up over in
Indio. True, it's got a few dings and dents, but it's still basi-
cally a beauty. She sudses the car's sloping back window, follows around to the sides, rubbing sap from the bottlebrush
off the hood, bending to wash the mag wheel covers.

    Everything she needs is right here in this trailer or she
doesn't need it, and if she ever wanted to she could just kick
out the blocks and off she'd go. Out of here. Carry her house

on her back like a turtle. Pull in her arms and legs whenever it damn well suited her.

She plays the water across the roof of the Camaro, then all over the car, running bubbles off with the spray. Finishing up with the dry chamois, her gaze wanders; she notices a woman hanging out wash from that old turquoise singlewide down the hill, one of Simón's dilapidated rentals. A blue plastic laundry basket sits on a stump, and the woman crosses and recrosses the beaten-down yard, the clothesline sagging under the weight.

Oh Christ, Yo thinks, diapers. Millions of them. This is another world. She coils up the hose next to the faucet and slings the chamois into the bucket, but something catches her eye again. The woman—she looks younger than Yo; twenty-five, six maybe—bends down toward blankets on the brown grass, lifts a baby up against her breast, turning it this way, that way, a soft, unconscious rhythm of turning that becomes a dance, resolves itself into the shadow of a woman zagging across the landscape, as in a cave painting, burning herself into the landscape and into the moment in which the bucket still swings from Yo's hand.

March 17, 1983

       It's the night of the Casa Diva Fourth Annual Springtime Fashion Show. Marina arrives late, hoping there'll be so many guests she won't have to talk to anybody. She'll follow the example of iguana, hold herself still so she won't be seen against the intricacies of her background.

       There's plenty of color to get lost in. Flaming tiki torches everywhere and pink and orange lights beaming up into the palm fronds. A long buffet with a bar rests on trestles to the left beyond the pool, and a short runway stands to the right, festooned in crepe paper and artificial flowers. Marina picks up a margarita from the bar when the bartender's back is turned and makes her way carefully past the boisterous and perspiring mariachis in their hot wool suits to the folding chairs set up around the runway.

       She's come, really, to see Gilberto. Mac said the fashion show was Gilberto's time to shine. Marina wanted to see that shining. Some of the fading she had already seen: a cold that turned into bronchitis that turned into pneumonia. She sips her drink, begins to feel the pulse of the guitarrón through the thin soles of her sandals.

She had offered to help with the food, but Mac insisted on caterers because he liked to be a guest at his own party. "I even like my guests to be guests at my party," he'd added, giving her a light, embarrassed hug.

"Well," Gil had said to her, "Don't think, girlfriend, that you can help with my makeup because one glance at you convinces me I'd be better off asking the caterers. Natural beauty is so tiresome." He had looked about, his expression momentarily bright, fancifully wicked.

"Salsa? Chips?" asks Mac, sitting down next to her and offering forth two bowls. "Just like mother used to make. Speaking of which, did we find a sitter for the wee one?"

"She's at Lupe's," she says, scooping up salsa and biting into a chip. "It feels really good to be with grown-ups."

"Not exactly, dear. Dream on. Not many here could qualify for that honor. Ah, but here's one. Marina, this is Salvador, Gil's tribal brother. Sal's a grown-up."

Salvador shakes her hand somberly, sits down in a folding chair in the row behind. Mac offers him salsa, then drifts off. Marina can feel this man's waiting presence. His eyes. He's expecting her to speak, to exert herself to start and maintain a conversation. She looks at the stage, resisting.

"I'm not arrogant; I'm just shy," he says.

She turns around to face him.

"Isn't that what you were wondering?"

"What makes you think I was wondering?"

He laughs. "That's one for you."

"I'm sorry. You're Gil's brother, and I would never . . ."

"We're both Cahuilla." He checks her eyes for understanding, then adds, "Agua Caliente Band."

"Indian, you mean."

"Same ones that own the land you're sitting on right now, Marina. It is Marina? Marina what?"

"Marina. Marina Lomas."

"Well, Marina Lomas, our tribe owns the land you're sitting on, as well as the hot mineral stream running under it. That's why we're the Agua Calientes. Named by the conquistadores. We used to call ourselves the Kauisik, not that anybody ever asked."

"My grandmother was Indian . . . on my father's side," she says, watching preparations on the runway.

He laughs. "Seems like everybody's got an Indian grandmother these days. Where you from anyway?"

"Oh, I've lived lots of places."

He waits. "You don't talk much, do you?"

"When I have something to say."

"I'm starting to believe in that Indian grandmother. Can I get you anything? Food, another margarita?"

When he returns with fresh margaritas he sits down next to her, taking off his cowboy hat and settling it on his knee. "How do you know little brother?"

"I work for him."

He raises dark eyebrows.

"I'm a housekeeper, a maid really. Mac calls me a housekeeper." She laughs. "Why do I have the feeling you're going to say, 'But you don't look like a maid'?"

"You mistake me. There's honor in all work," he says. Then smiles. "Well, damn. I sound just like my grandfather. No, worse. I sound just like my father. The truth is, I *was* going to say you don't look like a maid."

"But I *am* a maid."

"Okay, that's fine. No offense." Then he smiles. "You know it's usually people telling me I don't look like an Indian. Guess I should have learned something from that. You really don't say much, do you? Shy's my guess. So tell me how come a person shy as you has got this shy guy doing most of the talking?"

"You don't look shy," she says.

"You got a sense of humor too, I see."

"I was starting to wonder."

"As bad as all that?" he asks, extending an open pack of cigarettes.

"Why Salvador Greenfeather," interrupts Gil, standing tall in a gold lamé evening dress with frost tulle collar, "are you hitting on our Marina?"

"Oh Christ, is that really you, Gilberto?"

"Well darling, let's just say it's one of me. You're staying for dancing after the show, aren't you? Of course, no heterosexuality allowed. "Tisk, tisk. Naughty, naughty. Oh my, I mustn't miss my curtain. Ta."

When he turns, he collides with a woman in a blue silk shirt, gray linen pants, and short dark hair. "Yo, I'm so glad you came. Do you know these fascinating people?"

"I know Sal," she says, extending her hand, then turning

to Marina adds, "And this fascinating person is my newest neighbor."

Marina takes her hand. "Your neighbor?"

"Vista Coachella, world's most dilapidated trailer park. I'm in the Airstream just above you and a little west."

"The red sports car."

"Flamboyant little dyke," says Gil. "What's a mother to do. I tried my best to raise her right. Listen, I've got to run, girlfriends. Sal, I include you. One can always hope." And he glides gracefully off toward the runway in gold heels.

March 18, 1983

1 ✐ Marina holds her sponge under the tub faucet and squeezes until rivulets of water run between her fingers. She's cleaning the Bette Davis suite, having finished up in Lauren Bacall. Hortensia, the other maid, will work a few hours restoring order in the patio after the fashion show last night, then take what's left of her day off. So Marina will have to work faster, though something inside her keeps saying slow down. Why is that?

Usually she's a fast worker, but all morning long she's had the persistent feeling she's moving through deep water. She shakes Ajax onto her sponge and begins rubbing slow circles of cleanser all around the bathtub. Probably she feels this way from being up late, drinking. From being with people again. Things she's not used to doing. She rinses the grit out slowly, sending waves of water breaking against the back of the tub. Then she stands to face the bright mirror ringed with movie-star lights. She leans into it, almost speaks.

Picking up the sponge, she scatters cleanser into the sink, scrubs, pauses, remembering in her body the feeling she had last night when she saw for the first time women dancing together, Yolanda dancing with a woman, with women, how Marina had found herself watching in a sidelong way while Salvador talked on and on, the muscles in his jaw hardening as he talked about land, about change, about the tribal chief dying and his successor deciding to burn down the cere- monial building, the sacred bundle, ending the cultural life of his people. Like a mass suicide, Salvador had said, looking away, tensing the muscles in his jaw like a movie-star hero.

More like murder, she'd thought.

The whole thing made her a little restless, a little angry, especially because she could feel beneath Salvador's words a drift toward claiming her sympathy, an urgency reminding her of David and his needs. And she wanted to jerk away from this situation, from all male imploring. She wanted to return to her lizard self, concealed, transformational, soli- tary.

And yet in this very mood, something else was happen- ing inside her, some unaccountable seeking going on that she was hardly conscious of, and it had to do with Yolanda and the way the dark silk of her shirt had made a diagonal fold across her back, how the rich incline of her lower back modulated into full hips moving to music. Had to do, per- haps, with moonlight. All of this claimed Marina in some way that Salvador sensed, that caused his tone to become more urgent, insistent over the music.

Finally Marina had seen Yolanda moving away from her partner, her group of friends, walking her way, coming to stand at her side, and when Marina turned to her against the drag of Salvador's attention, Yolanda held out her arms and said, "Dance, neighbor?"

Part of her objected to the tone, the faint attempt at humor, and yet she found herself rising to her feet like a woman summoned out of her sleep for some ancient purpose.

At first there was confusion, a physical blundering about who would lead, who follow, and then simply their arms held each other inside a charged field of warmth and perfume, Yo's hand light against her spine. They might have been dancing on the surface of a pond.

She raises her eyes back to the mirror now, asking, "¿Quién eres, quién eres ahora?"

2 ✐ The woman in the bed is waiting like a dry root for the water to reach her through intricate conduits of irrigation. Is it a dream or does she hear the sound of a tool searching through earth, the scratch-scratching quest for the root of things, reasons, causes, the deep thing buried in the dark?

Eliana Townsend's head gives a jerk and she knows she has been listening to Crescencio's hoe moving through the arid landscape of her dream. She looks past the foot of her bed at the flowers he planted where she could see them and she feels this elixir of gratitude as a substance, as medicine.

The house is quiet. George left an hour ago for the office. Sometimes she wishes him gone, feels his mind—when he sits by her bed—gone somewhere else, driving toward the office. Then when he is finally gone she feels something not quite like loneliness. It is not that she minds being alone but that she minds being alone with this stranger, her illness.

She studies her hands lying on the coverlet, the dark blotches she has tried to ward off with creams and dispel with bleaching lotion: there nonetheless. Ugliness is moving into her body, lo feo, a process that has somehow speeded up now that her attention is elsewhere, fixed on this invader who has taken up residence inside herself, consuming all her energy.

She lifts one hand to make sure it is still possible. Lets it fall. Remembers her mother when the cancer had crept into her lungs, remembers the heave of her chest, the fatigue, remembers the day she consented to the bedpan, and all the other indignities that followed.

Remembers also the mother denied, her birth mother, the brown woman—girl really—who had moved on with the workers when the crops were picked.

And gradually—as Eliana thinks these thoughts—the oranges outside her window in Palm Springs grow into the oranges surrounding her child house in the Imperial Valley, the oranges bigger then, the sky bluer. She feels herself falling into the arms of her real mother, la morena, knows she is learning the art of self-comfort, allows her child-self both mothers. They sit, the three of them, three women in chairs under an orange tree, listening to the sounds of irrigation.

Her eyes snap open. There is reason to be vigilant, and yet she is not sure why. Perhaps if she yields to this scene, to her mothers and to the scent of oranges, she will have to relinquish some of her rights here, the ones that accrue to her as the wife of George Townsend. The right to say and to determine. The right to run her house and her body.

Never again will she go to the hospital. Would not permit it. Last time she had awakened in the night with fever, didn't know where she was, what the tubes were that held her in place. She had pulled them all out of her arms, fallen to the floor because the night nurse had left the rail down. In the morning they had scolded, x-rayed her hip and ribs, turning her mercilessly on the cold steel table as if she were a cadaver for study and not a living woman, a person with rights.

She was not fooled by any of this, deceived into thinking that if she were good she would become well. She had tried that. Spent a lifetime trying that. Had raised her two daughters, supported her husband in his career and consoled him in his terrors, had volunteered in the community, had done everything they had said to do, and where had it all led? To a young man in a white coat telling her she had emphysema, to another saying she probably had cancer, to another saying it was all in her head.

It had led straight to this morning, in which she lay on her side in a rented bed, nine bottles of pills on the nightstand, scribbled directions from George, her only comfort the steady, devotional sound of earth being turned over around her roots, the wild scent of oranges.

3 ⌀ Biscuit Reed could never explain to anybody why she likes to come here. She pulls her little fawn-colored Mercedes convertible into a space in the shade of a jacaranda

tree and looks up at the Spa Hotel, notes the peeling pink paint, the patches of concrete fallen away from earthquakes.

Indians, she knew, never could keep up anything. But the spa itself is beautiful and clean, probably because it's a religious place and all. Biscuit likes to approach it in an attitude of respect. From the trunk she lifts her pearl-white Samsonite cosmetic case and heads for the entrance. The man who opens the door for her doesn't look Indian but you never could tell these days.

Her heels make a little clicking sound down the hall. She can hear silverware tinkling, plates rattling in the Spa Hotel Restaurant, a place she would never eat again. The lettuce had been yellow and the fry bread made her sick. Harold said what do you expect. Biscuit had always tried to keep an open mind whenever he was not around and to do more or less exactly what she wanted.

She hands the woman at the spa desk a twenty-dollar bill and stares, while the woman makes change, into the dark part dividing her blond head in two. It's important to keep yourself up, which is why Biscuit has come here today.

From the locker attendant inside she accepts a white terry-cloth robe and a pair of white plastic scuffs, along with her key. She looks at the number to see if it means anything. Some people believed numbers were magic or dangerous, but Biscuit could never keep straight which numbers meant what. Nine was good; she knew that. But her number was seventy-one which added together meant eight. Money, she guessed. Eight meant money.

But that's not what she has come to find out about. She turns the little key in the lock and puts her purse inside. Not that she doesn't trust the people here, but you never knew. Inside the dressing room she changes into her bathing suit, puts on the robe, locks up her clothes. Looking down at her feet in the scuffs she notices her Fire and Ice polish is chipped.

And weren't feet the oddest things anyway? Hers looked yellow and calloused, kind of like chicken feet, come to think of it. Without wanting to all at once she remembers the day she ran outside and saw her mother swinging a chicken until its neck snapped. Now why would she think of that?

Inside the sauna she sits on the wooden bench and hopes the woman across from her will not notice her chipped toenail polish. She herself judges people by such things though she knows perfectly well what really matters is what's inside a person.

Unfortunately what's outside requires constant tending, which is what she had come to ask about. That facial rejuvenation thing. If it's time and all.

Eliana's so sick she really hasn't wanted to bother her about it, ask her advice. So she's come here to ask Nukatem, the Indian god who lives inside the healing waters and who she has read about on all those little framed stories and pictures that line the way into the Spa Hotel Restaurant, where she is never going to eat again.

Come to think of it, she really should bring Eliana to the spa when she gets to feeling a little better because people have been coming here for hundreds of years, to these very waters, which have thirty-two different minerals in them. One or the other of them is sure to be exactly what Ellie needs.

She takes one last deep breath of the eucalyptus steam and gets to her feet. She's ready. She walks past the television playing "General Hospital," past the polished urns of coffee and plastic pitchers of juice, past the low table of women's magazines, and through the arches leading to the baths. Everything marble. Like for royalty.

The attendant pulls open the plastic curtain surrounding one of the tubs. This woman is definitely Indian. She has that look about her like she knows something but is not about to say what. Wouldn't she be surprised to know that Biscuit believes in all this probably more than she herself does? That she has come here so Nukatem can help her decide a life or death kind of question?

Behind the closed curtain she approaches the deep tub, lays her robe on the white plastic chair, averting her eyes from last year's tummy tuck. She gives the rumbling water her undivided attention, using what she has learned from the tape on living in the moment. The surface jumps with tiny waves moving in every direction, colliding with each other, casting up spray like a miniature riptide.

Slowly Biscuit Reed descends the stairs, takes a deep breath, and lowers her troubled body into sacred waters. Nukatem, she says, yielding herself up to the mystery.

March 25, 1983

Marina stands three coins on end in the slot on the last washing machine and slides them in. Water begins spilling out like a tiny waterfall. This time she knows what to do and moves with assurance.

The first time at the laundromat she had not understood about the money and the machines. A battered woman in a red change apron had come at her, weight rolling from side to side like a foundering ship, her shoes crumpled down on the inside, her knees flung together in perpetual disagreement. She had shown Marina how to stand the quarters on end, defying gravity. Demonstrated the soap machine, saying push in the coin slot and pull it all the way out. When the soap failed to drop, she had said in a whisky voice, her tone both kind and admonishing, "You don't know what all the way means, do you, honey."

Everything had seemed to mean itself and something more, then. The hand-lettered sign that read: "Not responsible for loss or damage." The Muzak playing "Once I Had a Secret Love."

Today she is just a young mother doing the wash. Everything will agree to be itself and nothing more. She measures half a cup of Fab into a machine, then empties the diapers from the pail into the tub, fills the bleach dispenser with Clorox from home. Her two other machines have begun clicking and sloshing through their cycles. Carolina squirms and slides down in her infant seat. In a minute she will need her playpen.

Through the plate glass window Marina notices a strange tint to the sky, too early for sunset, something suspended, hushed. Sepia tones. In Juárez it might mean rain, in Des Moines it definitely would. Here she doesn't know. She dashes to the car, just in case, throws open the trunk, pulling out everything she might need in the next couple of hours, slams it shut, and hurries back in.

An old woman like a twig, the only other person in the Immaculate Conception Laundromat on Saturday at dinnertime, looks at her with faint disapproval and turns back to her *Life* magazine. The small, scruffy dog curled up in her lap raises his head momentarily, as if to ask a question, then reconsidering, lowers it.

Carolina begins emitting the little sounds of complaint that mean she has been sitting too long. Marina sets up the playpen and puts Carolina inside on all fours, hands her a teething biscuit.

The first washer begins to thump and wobble. The old woman looks at her, the dog glowers. Under their scrutiny she lifts the lid and pulls the sheets around a little, closes the lid. A regular muffled beat begins, the load strikes its point of balance, continues its cycle. Marina pulls an orange plastic chair up to the playpen, flips through a grubby copy of *Good Housekeeping.*

A man walks in with two pillowcases of dirty clothes and dumps them into four machines. He wears no socks, strips off his shirt and throws it in, stands in his undershirt thinking, then starts slapping his pockets, slowly at first, then with deliberation, as if the slapping would produce the quarters. Marina keeps reading.

The old lady says, "Here young man, I've got change," giving Marina a look that accuses.

Something about the light in the curve of the man's ear as he turns reminds her of David. Nothing else, just the illumination of blood. And she thinks of her own blood. Blood from her nose, the thin trickle the first time he hit her, and sorry he was so sorry it would never happen again. Until the next time. And the next. His blows becoming refined, confining themselves to the soft parts of her body that didn't show, extravagant yellow-blue-purple flowers, for her eyes only. Or for his. To the world, they were lovers and partners, traveling together always, she advising him about style and design in his business.

And she allowed herself to believe what others saw, kept a secret room inside her skull where pain could blossom in the dark. When she told him about the child it seemed his happiness was complete. He would be the best of fathers, he would cherish them both. She became again the Mexican princess, the one he had married. Not the American bitch who had mysteriously supplanted her. He was the same gallant, capable man who had courted her off and on for almost five years, courting at the same time the whole family. He had played chess with her father, drunk cognac, told stories, bought tile for his large company in the Midwest. Brought her American mother presents: dresses, electrical appliances, chocolates, records. American mysteries for herself, books of poetry.

When a car driven by a drunk left Marina motherless, he had grieved with her father, with herself, waited patiently until she finished her art degree at San Luis, turned twenty-one. Her father had been consoled by the marriage, by the knowledge that now David would take care of her. This fair Cortés.

But as the pregnancy wore on, his patience wore thin. He hit her with words, then with hands. She slept in the nursery on a pile of quilts, the door locked, while she waited for Carolina to be born. And for a while after the birth he had fallen in love with fatherhood.

But Marina already knew, already was saving maps, money, advice, waiting for the time when he would be away long enough that she could transform herself, slough the skin, disappear into this vast country from which her mother had come.

She looks at the three machines. All the red lights have gone out. Carolina is weaving her fingers into the mesh netting, about to get caught, about to register displeasure. Marina pulls her gently by her leg to the center of the playpen and winds up her musical pillow. Then she yanks open the door of a dryer and begins emptying the washers, giving each article of clothing a quick shake.

She puts in five dimes, turns the knob. The man with ears like David's strides shirtless out into the orange air, and she becomes again the woman of no history at all. Just the young mother reading a magazine while her clothes dry. Simply that.

The old lady rises carefully on stick legs and begins pulling from the dryer little electrically charged balls of clothes that snap and spark. The dog trots around, sticks his nose through the mesh of the playpen, snuffles, making Carolina laugh.

Some of the old lady's clothes are not quite dry. She searches her coin purse for another dime, stares at Marina until she can claim her attention. "Well, just look at that now, will you? Making friends, those two. Say, you got change for a solid quarter? I'm a dime short." She holds out the coin.

Marina's digging around in her bag when the dog starts barking, backing away from Carolina, racing left, then right, growling low, showing teeth and black gums, running to the door, yapping, backing away, dashing at the windows, yelping.

"It's coming, it's coming. Get a grip now," the woman says, holding out her arms, like a circus performer, for the little dog to jump into.

A trembling and chattering starts in the washer lids, then the concrete floor begins moving in waves as if they are all being swallowed by a monster. Marina grabs up Carolina from the playpen and sits on the bench, tucking her in close, hunching over her, sheltering her with her body, making a shield with her rib cage.

Finally the roaring and rattling slows and stops; the floor slows and consents to lie flat. The old lady looks, with interest, with admiration, at the dog in her arms, says, "He always knows, that one. He can feel it. Just before it happens."

Marina knows exactly what she means.

March 26, 1983

Yo tends to have crazy dreams whenever there's an earthquake. After surviving a 3.8 on the Richter scale, and three aftershocks, this is what she dreams. She's swimming in the aquifer, doing a slow, meditative crawl under the streets of downtown Palm Springs, but at the same time she's standing on the corner of Ramon and Palm Canyon watching herself stroking along in this regular, rhythmic way. Kick, kick, breathe; kick, kick, breathe.

Every now and then the swimming self comes up for air, once for an ice-cream cone at Baskin Robbins. Then down she ducks again and swims some more. Suddenly everything changes; there is a heave, a deafening whirling-sloshing sound as if she is going down an enormous drain.

She sits up in bed, her heart beating like the swamp cooler. Matter of fact it *is* the swamp cooler she hears, and she tries to separate out her heart from the machine. It's four A.M. and she is wide awake. Damn! And Sunday too. Could have slept till ten if she'd wanted.

She flings back the covers, pulls up the bedroom blind all the way. The moon fixes her with its strange, imperative spotlight. Should have known: earthquake, full moon, la locura.

She looks down the hill to see if maybe Marina is awake, but no, everything dark and quiet there. Yolanda is watching for signs but there don't seem to be any.

Well fine by her. She flops back into bed. What did she need with a straight woman anyway? With a baby, no less. Yo was traveling light, had everything she needed right here. Good job, nice car, la familia.

Having thought of her job, she thinks of the blood samples she's been seeing. Low T-cells, high levels of class B lymphocytes, and high alpha interferons. Perfect recipe for AIDS, but these people are not gay and not IV drug users. Mostly they're old ladies. Old ladies from the body shop.

Connect the dots, Yo. She knows there's a shape here, if only she can find it.

She gets to her knees and slides open the window, smiles at the hag moon floating above three shaggy palms. It's a good time to hear los coyotes. She'll get up, kick off the swamp cooler, get the coffee going. Sleep's impossible, that's for sure. What a dream! Damn!

She gets up and pads down the hall toward the kitchen. Puts on the kettle for coffee, decides against instant, will—por Dios—make herself a cappuccino with the machine Corky gave her five years ago, to celebrate their second—and last—anniversary. Yo laughs ruefully, grinds beans with a loud rattling sound, packs the contents down hard in the little chrome cup, flips on the switch. Remembers at the last possible minute to screw the top on the water chamber, which, she now recalls, is why she hasn't used the machine in almost a year.

Coffee blew up all over the ceiling the last time. Great metaphor for her and Corky.

Es verdad that Yo's better off by herself, has been for nearly four years. Shoots a little pool, has her friends, her work, especially now with this mystery rising up out of all those test tubes of blood, a pattern, something to watch. Maybe a discovery to make.

She sits down at the kitchen table, gets up, remembering to flip the thermostat on the swamp cooler higher so the racket will stop. All she hears for a moment is the water trickling down from la máquina; a regular waterfall. Then as she sits in the stillness, listening through the open window, those other familiar sounds rise toward the surface: the coo of the mourning dove, the rasp of palm fronds, the rhet, rhet, rhet of the roadrunner, the lonesome bark of the fox.

How she loves all this, this place.

Loves it but she could leave if she had to, if she wanted to. Be gone in a flash. Out of here.

She glances over at the red switch on the machine. Blood red. All that life running around inside what we call blood, like a little city that never sleeps, a Coachella of fluids, and suddenly in her mind blood and water, the essential fluids, meet in a vortex of dream and mystery and work. She feels drenched, excited, exhausted. Unsure. Like something is about to happen. But what?

Coffee. She pours milk into a blue mug, steams it up with a screeching sound, adds the rich liquid. Life is good. She sips, is watching at exactly the moment the sun first tips over into the Indio Hills, flooding them with mocha java and scalded cream. She grabs her binoculars.

About six the light goes on in Marina's kitchen. Yo doesn't know what to do with all these feelings. Friday afternoon she ran into Marina in Immaculate Conception, helped her fold her sheets; her toilet kept overflowing, she said. Yo dropped by, fixed it, hoped to be offered a beer, a damn cup of coffee. Nada.

Lately she finds herself hanging around the Airstream, watching and listening for some sign or word from Marina. But she is not someone who waits, never has been; she likes to move, she likes the way before her clear. That night at the Casa Diva when they danced, heat started in her face and moved down, a sensation almost visible, a column of energy firing down her spine until finally it touched her in her deepest self.

Had Marina felt it too? Surely Yolanda had not just imagined this moment, surely it had surged and torqued between them, fired off by the mutuality of feeling.

A week had passed, and nothing. Smiles in front of the mailbox, cautious. Damn. Here it is Sunday. She usually washes her car Sundays, but now, the simplest everyday thing might mean something. Might look like something. She'd like to go back to just plain Sunday: wash the car, have dinner with Crescencio and Tía Josie. Iron her shirts. Get ready for Monday. No big deal. Just plain life.

She'd have to be crazy to get mixed up with a straight woman! Especially one with a baby, maybe a husband somewhere. Yo doesn't really know anything about Marina. Not facts anyway. Marina doesn't talk much, sends out silent warnings not to ask. Barriers and obstacles surround her. Flashing lights. Peligroso. Bridge washed out. Proceed with caution.

¡Basta! Time to go into the canyons. Whenever Yo's mind gets all balled up like this, that's what she does. Walks into one of the Indian Canyons. Gets clean. Clear. If she leaves now she'll beat the heat and be in time for Sunday dinner too. She takes her binoculars off the refrigerator, grabs a banana from the bowl on the table.

Half an hour later Yo hands three dollars to the Indian woman eating a Big Mac in the toll booth at the entrance to Indian Canyons and drives through the main gate, moving slow over corrugated roads toward Palm Canyon. The Agua Calientes didn't maintain the approach, maybe to keep traffic down. Still, it's cheap to come. So she feels welcome but like she has to be willing to deal with it. Living in the desert's like that. Everything's a little bit harder.

She parks in a swirl of dust. From the gift shop she hears the CD flute of Carlos Nakai. A hot breeze teases the feather headdresses, beaded purses, tomahawks, postcards festooning the entrance. A sign says to watch out for mountain lions.

She begins the descent: pavement at first with an iron handrail; then asphalt giving way to gravel, the rail disappearing. She follows the path into the oasis, where giant palms gather along the streambed, casting an inviting shade. Oasis. The word itself seems to send a breeze rustling through the shaggy trees. This shady ground where families congregated for hundreds of years: women washing clothes, weaving baskets, preparing food, children playing, elders conferring, telling stories. Community.

Now the tribe was strung out across the valley in the checkerboard pattern President Grant had created when the railroad came through. Now they lived in stucco houses with air conditioning, or in trailers with swamp coolers like her own. Some of them lived well, others not. Some of them lay in the cemetery she had passed on the way in.

Yo rests on the edge of a picnic table and takes a long drink from her canteen, listens to the birds rustling in the palms, making nests, finding food. Then she begins her steep journey into the far canyon, the way from here marked only by the language of landscape.

*

Yo has not packed anything for Sunday dinner, but it won't matter. Aunt Josie always brings plenty for everybody. She turns east onto Palm Canyon, winds through Cathedral City, speeds past malls, hotels, golf courses on either side of the highway. Everywhere flamboyant billboards proclaim luxurious houses and condos: Vista del Oasis, Shadow Hills, Rancho del Oro, La Quinta Mirage.

58   She turns south on 74 and begins climbing into the Santa Rosa Mountains. The steep road zigs and zags, but Yo could drive it with her eyes closed. She makes a hairpin right onto an unmarked road that soon turns to dirt and dust, passes an abandoned ranch, half-burned, a small yellow house with window boxes, and then pulls up in front of the house she was born in, a house built of scrap wood and stone and tile and bottles, a room here, a room there, a patchwork patio off the back made of mountain stone and squares of tile, of old marbles and Mexican coins and keys to forgotten locks. Beyond that, the vegetable garden. In front, her cousin Jaime's shiny new black Chevy pickup with red trim parked next to her father's old Ford, both watched over by the ironic and mismatched headlights of her dead uncle's black truck, the truck her father knew could be fixed up one day, if only Jaime would take his advice.

One day she will buy Crescencio a new truck, casual. Just park it in front of the house. Toss him the keys. No big deal.

Tía Josie calls to her from the front porch, motioning her to hurry. "I brought over tamales, mi'ja. Your favorite." She pulls her tight against the clean smell of her cotton dress. They walk inside, their arms around each other.

"Daughter," acknowledges Crescencio Ramírez with a nod.

Since her mother died—almost five years ago now—he has assumed the role of the disapproving parent, never having performed it during her lifetime. As if he must keep his daughter's mind on some assigned task, unsure himself what it is. She hugs him, then hugs her cousin, who is rising to greet her from a chair in a dim corner.

"It's all ready," says Tía Josie. "Jaimito, bring that blue chair into the kitchen. We got barbecue ribs, mi'ja, and flour tortillas fresh made. Tomatillos from the garden."

Yo gets the Dos Equis from the refrigerator. They all sit down at the kitchen table. Jaime reaches for the tortillas, but a glance from his mother freezes his hand. Crescencio sits with eyes closed. Yo looks into her lap, thinks, Oh Christ, here we go.

"I'm getting old, Father," says Crescencio. Yo looks up, but her father is staring into his plate, eyes closed. "I'm getting old and I want to see the people I love settled down and happy and maybe having kids, if it should please you. Right now I'm thanking you about the food. But this other is on my mind too—I got to admit—in the name of the Father, the Son, and the Holy Ghost, amen."

They cross themselves and reach for the food. Yo says, "And what was all that about, Crescencio?"

"I'm still your father," he says, buttering a tortilla thoughtfully. "Is that how you address your father?"

"I'm not going to have kids. No way. Not in this lifetime. I've explained all that to you." She takes the platter of ribs from Tía Josie.

"Oh you've explained all right," he says. "But you don't know everything there is to know. Not yet you don't."

"Well I wouldn't mind seeing Jaime settle down, that's for sure," says Aunt Josie, taking the husks off her steaming tamale. "This time married. But first he's got to meet the right girl."

"That's right," says Jaime between bites on his rib, "and I ain't met her yet."

"Me neither," says Yo.

"That supposed to be funny?" her father asks, a bite of tamale suspended on his fork.

"The girl's got to live her own life," Tía Josie says. "It's a cinch we can't live it for her." She laughs. "I might want to try. But this one's hers."

"We each got to live our own," says Jaime, still gnawing. "Like, Tío, there are things I could tell *you* about how to live." He looks meaningfully into Crescencio's eyes.

"Don't start in with me about working in no golf course, Jaimito. I have my customers and my ways and I like things the way they are."

"Twice as much, man. You could make twice as much working with me on the golf courses. And get bennies. You know bennies?" He is gesturing with his rib bone. "Benefits, I'm telling you. Health. Retirement. Los dientes." He touches a gold incisor, as if to make his point.

"But what about my customers, hijo? I got customers. Some I had for ten, twenty years." He slices into one of his own tomatoes.

"They don't care about you, old man. Esos gabachos in suits."

"We got it worked out, Jaimito. Don't you worry about that. We got it worked out. And that's another thing. Josefina, Mr. Townsend, he wants to know can you take care of his wife weekdays. Come to the house. Clean a little. Not much."

"I'm retired. Como tú sabes, Crescencio. Two years since I worked."

"She don't need to work," says Jaime, helping himself to a tortilla and slathering it with butter. "I take care of her."

"You don't take care of me. I take care of myself. And I'm always going to. Gary Luna left me that social security of his."

"That's because Gary Luna was a good esposo, looked out for you, hermana. Gary Luna was a man. To tell the truth, I miss him. I can't get a friend like him these days. They don't make them like that no more. You should fix up his truck, Jaimito. That's a good truck. You could use it."

"I got a truck, Tío."

"The truck of your father, I'm talking about. Don't let nothing go to waste, Jaime. Your father never did. Those Cahuillas used everything God gave them, made shovels out of the palm fronds, ate the fruit, roofed their houses with the leaves, sewed their clothes. Nothing got lost."

"If you hear what you're saying, tus propias palabras, hermano, then you know Gary Luna's not lost either. He's right here, same as those palm trees. People like Gary, they know how to come and go, is what I'm telling you. But you got to listen for them. They're not going to do it all."

Jaimito is staring into his plate. Yo's mouth is twitching a little at the corners. Crescencio is staring at his sister, this woman who can say things that make him want to cross himself while she just goes on eating her tamales. Crescencio is trying to get back to the main point, but Josefina has made him lose it momentarily with her talk about the dead.

"Gary Luna," he says, picking up the thread of his story, "was a good friend, and a good husband, and a good father. ¿Verdad?" He looks at Jaime. "Because he knew how to watch out for people. That's what I'm saying. Now some people in this world don't have anybody like Gary Luna. Nobody's taking care of them. ¿Entiendes?" His gaze falls now on Josefina. "Bueno, this lady I'm trying to tell you about, she can't take care of herself. Está enferma. All the time. And she loves the flowers. Somebody's got to look after her." He picks up a rib, looks at it curiously, then sets it down. Sits staring into his plate. Nobody says anything.

Finally he looks up. "You know how they do, those gringos. Somebody gets sick and next thing you know they're checking them into the damn hospital so the doctors can kill them." He glances out the small window, sets down his fork. "So Josefina, can I tell Mr. Townsend you'll come?"

"Seems to me you got a lot on your mind today, hermano, a lot of big plans for everybody." She laughs. "Yes, you can go ahead. Tell him I'll try it out and see do I like it. Trial basis, like on the TV."

Yolanda watches her father relax back into his chair and thinks maybe she is not the only one in this family crazy in love.

April 2, 1983

It's the morning of the Agua Caliente Band's Spring Powwow, and Yo is looking out the window for Gil and Mac in the "lady car," a long white Lincoln Town Car with white leather upholstery. Gilberto says it's just a little something for the tastefully tasteless. They will pick her up and then Marina and the baby. "It's more ecological," Mac had said on the phone the night before, then laughed wickedly. "Besides, what are friends for?"

Well, she is going to play it very, very cool. She lets the curtain fall into place and begins pacing back and forth across the confined kitchen. Catches herself, decides to water her pots, is pondering a case of needle shedding on her biggest cactus when she hears the lady car stopping on the lower road to pick up Marina. She turns off the water, coils up the hose. Damn, she can't remember what she meant to bring. A quick collective swing through the trailer, an adjustment to the swamp cooler, and they pull up in front.

With Salvador Greenfeather. For whom she has never had very much use. And vice versa, judging from the sour expression on his face when he turns to greet her. He's in the front seat with Mac and Gil. She slips into the back seat with

Marina and the baby. Mac tips Yo a reasonably inconspicuous wink and then moves the great car forward, on toward the Indio fairgrounds.

In less than twenty minutes they are all milling around behind the trunk of the car, deciding on gear. Marina has brought the stroller but is not sure it will work in all this sand and dust, and Gil is saying he doesn't need the wheelchair.

He brandishes his silver-handled cane and says, "If Carolina doesn't have to get in her stroller, then neither do I."

Mac gives him a skeptical look. "But how are you feeling? I mean, how are you really feeling? You're tiresome when you're being stoical, Gilberto."

"The way I really feel." He sets his cane into the sand. "The way I really feel. Well, it's powwow and I have always adored powwow because it's such a fantastic opportunity for dress up. But I have decided quite sensibly not to enter the Men's Jingle Dress Competition. At least not this year. Sal, my sweet, are you entered?"

Salvador is struggling gallantly into the backpack designed to hold babies and telling Marina about the spiritual underpinnings of powwow. Yo smells fry bread. Carolina yells when Marina puts her into the backpack but quiets down as they make their way toward the entrance. There are a lot of white-haired Anglos dressed in pastels, wearing thin-soled shoes dyed to match, people who usually golf on Sundays or ride the tram up for dinner on Mount Jacinto without ever stepping off into snow. They have come here today for a cultural experience.

Too bad they will not all have the benefit of Salvador Green-feather as interpreter. He is really warming to the task, as if he is the last Indian on the face of the earth. The Cahuillas used to own the whole Coachella Valley. Well, not exactly *own*, he corrects himself. Indians didn't believe anybody could *own* the land, though evidently Sal has no difficulty believing his band *owns* the Palm Springs Spa Hotel, as well as the mineral springs under it, for which they charge entrance fees, towel fees, mud facial fees, and body wrap fees, freeloading off women's cosmetic anxieties with the best of them. Not to mention controlling several thousand acres of prime Palm Springs real estate with hundred-year ground leases.

Yo is glad they have what they have, and she does not object to Sal's self-contradiction. She herself embraces paradox, especially when it comes to spiritual matters. Having abandoned Catholicism long ago, in times of crisis she always finds herself praying aloud to the Virgin of Guadalupe; she sometimes lights candles, crosses herself in the car.

It's perfectly possible to believe nobody owns land and that you've been cheated out of yours. What she does object to is Sal's tone. That high moral tone used to thinly disguise grievance: a whine.

Maybe she had been spoiled by Gary Luna, half Cahuilla himself, who just kept to the path. That was all. Did not make pronouncements. Sal would probably not consider her uncle a tribal brother at all. Just another breed. But really wasn't everybody by now pretty much mestizo? Being Mexican meant—at least in theory—you were half Indian. So what was she, Yolanda Ramírez. Chopped liver? And the Indians and the Mexicans had intermarried here for hundreds of years. Which meant Salvador Greenfeather probably had a whole lot of Mexican blood in him. If blood was the issue.

Personally, Yo couldn't think of blood in metaphoric terms anymore. Blood was blood. Describable, quantifiable, essential, compelling life fluid.

But they have arrived at the ticket booths. Sal gallantly springs for Marina's ticket. Mac rolls his eyes. Gil pauses over a bolo tie of unique design at the first table of Indian crafts. Salvador is turning up his nose at machine-made beadwork and leather goods from Taiwan, little feather-trimmed drums that say Palm Springs Powwow on them. Cahuillas historically are not a drumming tribe, he explains.

Just then they hear drumming. Three old men stand on a raised platform wearing elaborate headdresses, flanked on either side by drummers. A crowd gathers. It's getting a little hot. Yo wishes she had not left her baseball cap in the car. Carolina, under her sun bonnet, is staring up at the men in feathers and scrunching her fists in a gesture that seems to mean: hand them over, quick.

Salvador is explaining in a stage whisper that the man in the middle would ordinarily be the net—the spiritual leader— but that they had no net because the last one, José Patencio (Yo notes the Mexican name), had resigned in a fit of pique over the decline of the purity of their culture and burned up all the band's ceremonial objects. This was apparently a heroic gesture.

What they were about to see and hear today would not be authentic, but it was the best that he, Salvador Greenfeather, could provide under the circumstances. First there would be bird songs and then the blessing by those elders not too generally pissed with the world to do it.

Bird Singers mount the platform, and Yo thinks of Gary Luna in his black feathers, but she is not going to mention—ever—her kinship in Salvador's presence. Finally he shuts up as the Bird Singers begin their song in Cahuilla, telling how the Bird People first came to the Coachella Valley and from there created the whole universe.

Gil leans close and whispers, "Aren't their dresses just too precious?" Sal glowers at him. Yo squeezes her friend's hand. It feels a little warm.

"You okay, Gilberto?"

He nods. Mac looks at him. He nods again.

The man standing in for the net has begun intoning. The drumming has stopped. He invokes the seasons, the corners of the universe. He thanks the creative force who created Mukat and Temayawut, who in their turn fashioned world, ocean, water creatures, and sky; he praises Mukat for sculpting people so skillfully out of black mud and for passing on to them the great gift of the Cahuilla language.

Yo relaxes into the morning and lets his song wing her up above the fairground and into a wider prospect, because in

the spaciousness of her own mind she knows he is now chant-
ing way beyond ground leases and mud packs; instead he is
calling on all the tribes, calling on everybody present to touch
the mineral spring of kinship they might have carried safely
68   to this spot.

April 10, 1983

Rain still drums on the roof of the ancient trailer. It started just after dinner and by two a.m. it has begun seeping under some of the riveted seams and dripping into buckets, bowls, whatever Marina can find to catch the rusty drops. At times gusts of wind howl and heave about the trailer. Marina remembers back through six weeks of *Desert Sun* headlines:

> *Palm Springs man rescued from flooded wash after half-inch of rain falls in Coachella Valley*

> *44-year-old woman missing and believed dead after car swept away by floodwaters near Thermal*

She remembers too what Yo said about that no-good Simón not using tie-downs on his rental trailers. Marina remembers Yo, thinks of her off and on through her days and nights like a song stuck in her head.

She slides out of the breakfast nook where she has been paying bills, traverses the short hall, and stands listening in the doorway of the narrow bedroom where Carolina sleeps in her playpen. She is breathing hard, had difficulty nursing at bedtime, has awakened every hour or so. Might be coming down with another cold, keeps getting them from the other kids at Lupe's.

Marina returns to the kitchen and sits in the nook, gazing out the window for the light burning in Yo's Airstream that she can perhaps not even see through the downpour. She needs a sentinel self, a guard dog for her heart. Pay the bills, she tells herself. She writes the date on a check, thinks she hears something beneath the wind, a different kind of moaning that has her on her feet and moving toward her child before she can even say to herself what she has heard.

Carolina is struggling to breathe, the side of her face hot and moist. She is still asleep, but Marina picks her up and, pulling the blanket around her, carries her into the lighted kitchen. She paces in the confined space. Paces thinking, wondering why she has chosen this spot out of the whole continent, when she might have lived in a place of primary colors and plentiful water. Child of the desert, she has predictably scurried to the subtly tinted landscape she matches. The predictability makes her think of David. David, who knows her.

Now she constructs a study of fear; it has perspective: the near and the far. Near, the loss of Carolina; far, the approach of David.

The bowl by the kitchen door has filled. She bends with her knees, keeping her back straight, guarding the baby's sleep;

rises, feeling the pull at her thighs, the disequilibrium of the bowl, the unlikelihood of the luminous face at the window, the rapping at the door: "Marina, Marina, are you all right?"

"I saw your light," Yolanda says, squeezing through the door, water flying from her yellow slicker as she slips out of it and takes the bowl of water from Marina's hand. "It's a bad one. Flash flooding all over the valley." She empties the water into the sink. "¡Ese Simón! Should have tied your damn trailer down. ¿Qué tiene la niña? ¿Está enferma?" She leans close, listening. "The asthma. Got anything for it?"

"No. ¿Verdad? Asthma? ¿Estás segura? She never had that before. Only colds, once an ear infection."

"We could try tea. The caffeine works like theophylline." She opens cabinets looking for something to boil water in. "You can tell because of the way she's breathing. Rattle on the exhale. Asthma. Probably the damn smog. Bad the last few days. Drifts down from LA. And now we got damp on top of that."

Carolina wakes crying, then trying to breathe, then crying, taking rapid breaths, coughing.

Yo makes the tea quickly, stirs in a little sugar, and cools it down with ice cubes, puts it into a bottle. Tests the temperature. "See if she'll take this. Otherwise I guess we better go to the hospital."

Marina sits down on the broken couch, cradling her daughter, offering the bottle. Carolina turns her head away, cries. Marina tries again. This time her lips close around the nipple; she takes a few quick sucks, followed by deeper ones.

"Whew," says Yolanda, "looks like it's going to work." She strokes the baby's damp hair. "She'll be all right."

"I didn't want to take her to the hospital."

"My father always says they kill you in the hospital. Matter of fact, my whole family says that. And here I am working in a damn hospital. Go figure." Yo is pacing quietly.

"It's good you knew what to give her."

"My Aunt Josie would have said lobelia tea made with skunk cabbage root, garlic, and a little rainwater. Maybe a wolf's liver, if you happened to have one on hand. She's a character. You really ought to meet her." She takes a deep breath. "I sure am talking a lot."

"It's all right," says Marina. "I was scared, too. Really scared."

Carolina has fallen into a rhythm: three long sucks and then sleep; three long sucks and then sleep. Marina eases her left elbow onto the arm of the couch for support, feels her body relaxing.

Yolanda is emptying buckets, bowls, pots; finds the mop, might be humming even, beneath the sound of the storm.

April 17, 1983

1 🖉 David stands in the kitchen lit only by moonlight, holding his briefcase. Every evening he arrives home a little later, putting off the time when he will stand here in this empty kitchen, like a man with tickets to a show that has been canceled. He puts his briefcase on the island next to the grill and turns on the light above the stove, a pale, noncommittal light. From a lower cabinet he takes out a bottle of Scotch, gets down two glasses. Puts one back. Takes three cubes out of the ice maker and drops them into the glass. Sound, like time, is magnified. As if he is living in a submarine. He runs a little water from the tap into his glass.

Then he picks up his briefcase, passing through the dining room, filigreed in light, down the hall, and into his study. Under the glow of the green desk lamp he sets his drink and opens his briefcase, takes out a thick envelope with the end torn off. He sips his Scotch and leans back in his swivel chair, easing the muscles bunched along his shoulders and up his neck. He already knows the contents of the envelope, the two pages he now spreads open before him.

He sips again. Two and a half months and three private investigators have passed, and now he has a long list of women located who are not Isabel. He does not like waiting and he does not like melodrama and he does not like private detectives, with their small talk and their excuses and their cheap suits. And yet he finds himself strangely dependent on them, unable to make a plan, his own timetable suspended.

Soon, very soon, he will have to make things happen. He is a man of action. Isabel knows this.

2 ✐ Gilberto sits up in bed, his heart pounding like the rainstorm. In the glow from the night light he sees the shrouded canary cage in the corner of the bedroom, senses the feathered shape huddled inside. Sweat breaks out across his forehead, his chest. He jumps at Mac's touch.

"Headache?" Mac asks.

"A dream."

Mac tugs gently at his shoulder. "It's the full moon. Storm and moon. Everybody on edge. Come on, let's cuddle."

"I'm worried. I'm worried about Dinah."

"I covered her."

"She might be having a heart attack in there."

Mac laughs.

Gil lies back down inside his partner's encircling arm. "It's not just Dinah," he says, arranging the covers.

"Are you going to tell me your dream?"

"You don't like to hear my dreams."

"Of course I do. It's my favorite thing, hearing your dreams. Tell me the dream."

"If you insist. The first thing I remember was this terrible screaming. I looked out the window and it was raining, like now. But I could see a goat outside in the flashes of lightning."

"A goat? In Palm Springs?"

"This is serious."

"I know that, dear. I'm sorry. Go ahead."

"The goat was in a pen. Something had jumped it, a wolf maybe. I could see it hanging there on the goat, tearing into his neck. The goat just stood there screaming, that's all it could do, just stand there in that locked pen screaming."

They lie together listening to the rain. Finally Gil wonders, "Can goats scream? I didn't think they could say anything. Like rabbits, you know? It was a terrible sound. I can still hear it."

"Rabbits can scream like crazy. My dad used to keep rabbits. They'd get out and the dogs would chase them. They'd scream bloody murder. And goats, you know goats make a noise. You've heard them at the fair."

"Well what do you think the dream meant?"

"You're the Indian," said Mac. "You tell me. You know about the dream time."

"That's right. Being around Sal too much makes me forget everything I know. Like if he's going to be the Indian then all I get to be is the drag queen. Would I go to all the trouble of being gay if I had to be just one thing all the time? I mean I could have bought a tie ten years ago and been done with it."

"And a gray suit."

"I hate gray."

"It doesn't suit you."

"Suits don't suit me."

"Oh, I don't know. That little pink number with the flowered . . ."

"Hush," says Gilberto, "this is serious."

"Everything's serious."

"Everything's serious, and everything's not."

"Gil, tell me about the dream."

"Well this is what I think. I think it meant that to be gay is to be a goat inside the pen of the white man's dead culture."

"I'm white," Mac observes.

"No you're not. You? You mean . . . ?"

"Yes, white. It's a true fact."

"You never told me that, Robert McVay. Well then I say that to be gay is to be a goat inside the pen of the straight man's dead culture."

"Thank you."

"You're entirely welcome."

"Because if you're going to be a goat," says Mac, "then I want to be a goat with you."

"You *are* a goat."

"If *you* are."

"I am. The dream tells me that. Only . . . Mac?"

"Yes, dear?"

"What are we going to do now? I don't think I want to just sit around doing my nails waiting for the wolves to come."

"Ask your grandfather, Gil."

"He's dead."

"You're an Indian, aren't you?"

"That's right, I am. Damn that Salvador Greenfeather." He closes his eyes. Mac watches him for so long in the glow from the night-light that he thinks Gil may have gone to sleep. But when he starts to cover him up, Gil stirs.

"Grandfather says the path is clear."

"Christ, you scared me half to death," Mac says, grabbing his heart. "What else does he say?"

Another silence, and then a voice Mac scarcely recognizes says, "Only one thing to do. You boys got to become shape shifters."

"Grandfather must have missed the last fashion show," said Mac, turning over and pulling up the covers.

  3 ⌀ George Townsend has been selling things for so long, and hustling to make a living, first for himself and later for his family, that it's hard for him to imagine anybody loafing through life and mistaking that for work. No wonder when he comes home at night dead tired and hoping maybe Josie has at least got dinner started that he is a little disgusted to see her sitting on the couch next to his wife, watching some TV show. Sitting there in house slippers brushing Ellie's hair. The two of them. Like a couple of girls. Sisters even.

He goes straight into the kitchen and opens the refrigerator and stares into it. Nothing you could call food, exactly. Tortillas, a tomato that probably Crescencio left, and some green chile peppers wrapped in damp paper towels. Two onions on the sink. A bowl of grapefruit on the counter.

Never mind, he'll make himself an omelette and maybe some hash browns to go with it. He searches in the lower cabinet for the omelette pan, hears laughter coming from the living room. Like she is somehow a guest in their house instead of a servant.

He can't find the omelette pan, knocks over a stack of pots, mutters under his breath, restacks them from large to small. An egg slips through his fingers and smashes on the floor, splattering everywhere. He wipes the linoleum on his knees, sees that the paper towel is filthy, that the kitchen floor— since he turned the housework over to Josie—has been getting dirtier and dirtier.

Never mind. He would speak to her later. Never speak in anger, he counsels himself in the mother's voice he carries inside. He takes a couple of deep breaths, slides open the drawer and looks through the tangle of implements for the potato peeler, sees corks, rubber bands, coupons, stamps, bits of string. Can't find the damn thing, flips open the dishwasher and there it is, leaning against unwashed cutlery.

Never mind. He rinses it under running water, watching rust streak the sink, dries the blade carefully and completely with a paper towel. Finds and washes his potato, carves out the eyes. Then finally, with the potato peeler flying over the potato, up to speed at last, it happens: a slice off the tip of his finger. As if he himself has become a potato. Mr. Potato Head.

He grabs a dish towel and strides into the living room in time to see Josie leaning close to his wife, fastening in her earring, while some fat Chinese detective is carrying on about his number one son. They don't notice him standing there, that he has come home from a hard day at the office. Don't notice the blood squeezing into the dish towel. That he is hungry, that he hasn't even had a chance to change out of his suit.

Yolanda positions Gilberto's arm where she can draw blood. He murmurs something as she works. Oxygen feeds up his nose from plastic tubing. She looks up at Mac, for translation.

"He wants to know if you're a vampire."

"A goddamn angel of mercy," she says, wiping his arm and inserting a needle. "That's what I am."

Gil looks away. His skin is pale and his arm feels thin and uninhabited. Like the body snatchers have got him. Yo fills one vial and starts in on a second. "You all right?" she asks Mac. He nods. She begins drawing blood into a third vial. "He eaten anything?"

"Not really. Can't keep it down."

"Umm." She seals the last vial and unwinds the tourniquet from his arm, kisses his hand, and tucks it back under the sheet. "Thank you, dear, for your lovely, lovely blood."

He speaks so low, from such a distance that she can't hear him. "He says the pleasure is all his," Mac interprets.

She puts the vials into her cart, makes some notations on his chart, gives Mac a quick hug, and goes rattling out the door.

Damn, he doesn't look good. And neither does Mac. She will stop by his room tonight when her shift's over, visit a little. Today, because she's got the eleven to seven shift, she'll have to take blood right on through the patients' lunch, a practice that seems barbaric to her but then, she is not in charge here.

Not that she'd mind being in charge. There are more than a few things she'd change around here, starting maybe at the top, with Mr. Meredith Disenhouse, and working on down to her own immediate supervisor, Silvia Cedeño, whose hair— like her mind—is teased and sprayed into immobility. But she'll have to talk with her soon enough.

When Yo gets back to the lab, Silvia is not around. Yo gets out her salami sandwich with lettuce, tomato, and onion in it, takes a bite, and begins placing the tubes of blood into the centrifuge. She wants to know Gilberto's latest T-cell count, but she also wants to know about Eliana Townsend, who is back in the hospital again, and a couple or three other body shop alumnae.

She'll have to get her facts straight before she tries talking sense to old Silvia, let alone to Harold Reed and the other administrative great white fathers who spend their days out there on the links improving their swings. It was Sil's job to see that their lives of play were never interrupted by the crisis of reality.

Yo flips the switch on the centrifuge, then she pulls open the bottom drawer of the desk the lab techs use and takes out a worn blue notebook that says on the cover in her own hand: YOLANDA RAMÍREZ. She flips it open, looking at the first column of figures, the column under the name ELIANA TOWNSEND. Next to that are four more columns and four more names.

82   She hums softly, waiting for the centrifuge to stop. Connect those dots, Yo, she tells herself and bites into her sandwich.

April 29, 1983

It's the third time in a week somebody has asked Biscuit Reed for books on this new disease carried by gay men. An hour ago she handed two books across the counter to a Hispanic-looking young woman with short hair who had what seemed to Biscuit an attitude problem. Instead of being grateful the woman had said, "Is that all you got?" Now she's hunched over the books writing down things in a blue notebook, muttering to herself. Very unfeminine.

Biscuit herself is well informed on this new disease. As the wife of the executive vice-president of the hospital it certainly behooved her to stay abreast of trends. Though Harold is not a doctor in his own right, he is the next best thing. Harold says this is a disease of gay people, drug addicts, and those kind of people. The rest of us have really got nothing to worry about.

Biscuit eyes the young woman and decides she must be a drug addict. That would explain her attitude. It was sad when people so young couldn't control their lives any better than that. When she hands the books back, Biscuit will be careful to wash up right afterwards.

She turns to the overdue notices, just getting lost in the

intricacies, when suddenly she looks up into the blaring eyes of the drug addict, who hands her back the two books, along with a piece of yellow paper. "What's this?" asks Biscuit.

"It's what I'll need next," says the young woman, just as

if Biscuit's sole purpose in life is to serve her. "*New England Journal of Medicine,* January issue. This year. That's the most important one. But all of them if you can manage it." Then she slaps that blue notebook against her hand once, twice, and strides out the front door.

Biscuit watches her red Camaro turn out of the parking lot. Biscuit has noticed that people who drive red cars tend to be rude. At the top of the yellow piece of paper she writes two question marks and slips it into Sally Augustino's "In" box. Then she shelves the two books next to the stack of magazines youngsters may not check out without a note from home. Now she will wash her hands. It's always better to be safe than sorry.

Carolina and Marina are both a little hyper. Sometimes Carolina is like that after day care at Lupe's. Stressed out. When that happens Marina just loads her into her backpack and walks with her into the Indio hills. The air and the flowers, the orange light making skinny shadows out of the Joshua trees, the gravelly rhythm of Marina's tennis shoes over the trail—all this calms them down.

The air is cooling, shadows lengthening. Birds skim in formation over the terra-cotta landscape. The weight of Carolina in the backpack has at last taken on the heft of sleep; her child skims the dreamscape.

For Marina, relaxation comes harder. She strides along, arms swinging, walking faster and faster up the incline. Leg muscles strain, breath becomes labored.

She is trying to outdistance her own preoccupations. She is trying not to think of Yolanda, the warmth of those accidental touches in the car at powwow, and again during the rainstorm, the quiet way she had helped her then with Carolina. When she thinks of Yo she sees color, she feels color in her body, feels her artist self stirring again, the world turning green.

She doesn't want to compare, not ever; still, when she thinks of David she thinks of whiteness, blankness, the eye of a fish cooked in a pan. Blind.

She shivers, walks harder. None of this makes any sense anyway. The one sleeping on her back is all she must think about now. La querida. Not herself, not Yo. She'll tax this body, make it work hard, so that her mind will quiet down.

But is it her mind she's trying to quiet?

¡Ya basta! This is not working! She is not going to get calm by walking into the hills. Not this time. What she needs to do is talk with Yolanda. She needs to talk with her right now. Stop avoiding.

But it's hard, with so much she must not say. So much she must. And for a moment she sees herself threading her way through a mine field, with no tools for help, only this heavy pack.

She circles back toward the trailer park, slow at first, then picking up speed. Out of the corner of her eye she glimpses something moving. Glances to see. A roadrunner, wild-eyed, ruffled, keeping pace for a while as if they shared a common concern, a destination, a purpose. Then finally it sheers off in the direction of the glow along the horizon, toward Indio, as if keeping an appointment.

Marina sees the light glowing in her own kitchen, but Yolanda's place looks dark. And yet her car is parked in its usual place, out under the palo verde. Yo has a ship's bell by the door decorated with strings of dried chiles and Indian corn. Plants in pots everywhere. Little lemon tree. Marina sounds the clapper against the bell once, leans against the side of the trailer breathing hard. Carolina startles. In a moment the door opens. The kitchen light flicks on.

"¿Estás durmiendo?" Marina asks. Yo's hair is awhirl with cowlicks.

"No, working. Thinking. Come on in. What time is it anyway? You okay? How's Carolina?"

"We're fine. We were out. . . . It's just that . . ." Marina stands with the baby, hesitant. Maybe she should leave. She glimpses sheets of graph paper all over the kitchen table, an open blue notebook, a green pen with the cap off. Old-fashioned; a fountain pen.

"¿Has comido?" Yo asks.

"Sí, sí, pero you go ahead. I think we better . . ."

They are standing in the dark. Yo leans toward her and kisses her tenderly on the mouth. Marina had not expected this and yet she has been waiting for this. There is a softness and a warmth that she could not have foreseen, that keep her rooted to the spot, uncomprehending.

Yo lifts Carolina out of the backpack, snugs her in close, sways with her. "She's out like a light. Shall I put her down? Can you stay a minute?"

Marina follows Yo down the hall to her bedroom, rousing herself enough to take mental pictures in the dim light so that later she can take them out and study them. The double bed covered by an Indian blanket, the Japanese lantern hanging over the two pillows, the cane-bottom chair with a pair of Levis tossed over the back.

Yo puts Carolina down on her bed, places the chair against the outside edge. Marina shrugs out of the child carrier, leaves it on the bed. The room smells of incense and of Yo.

As Marina starts down the hall following Yo, suddenly Yo stops and Marina glides into her, feels herself led, gently, somehow, into the small office where—within a dome of shadows and books—she feels Yo's arms around her and herself opening like a cactus flower, feels a hot current running inside her. They are kissing and her mouth is opening, and she is all over hot petals and sizzling liquids: agua caliente.

May 7, 1983

1 ✐ Crescencio holds the lemon to his nose and breathes in its sharp yellow aroma. This one's ready, he can tell. Sunday morning and he stands in his garden choosing for today's dinner. Yolanda brings somebody special.

Two fine tomatoes. He puts them into the basket with the limón. The lettuce is not too good. The sun gets warmer. Soon he must set up his covers made out of old shower curtains. Josie laughs at him but she's always happy to get the lettuce, he's noticed.

He wants the dinner nice, but still, he can't help worrying about Yolanda and the way she lives her life. Last time she brought somebody special was three, maybe four years ago. Called herself—¿cómo se llama?—Corky. Esas gringas with the names of dogs, dogs with the names of people. And his Yolanda, thrown away when that Corky got tired of her. No, he didn't like it, this way of living. De ninguna manera. Took his daughter a long time to get right after that.

What was wrong with fall in love with a good man, get married, have kids, he wanted to know? The green onions looked good. Maybe make a little salsa to go with the chips. Josefina was bringing chicken mole. He senses chocolate in the May air, the memory of his wife's mole sauce encircling him. He pulls up sprigs of cilantro, stares into his basket, missing his wife, su querida.

That's enough. He will make the salsa now. Should have made it this morning, to taste better for the afternoon, más sabrosa. He studies the tomato plants. Yo told him over the phone everything special.

But what if this woman, this Marina, turned out to be like esa Corky? Yo says she's a pocha, but still. For a moment he finds himself wishing his wife was here to deal with all of this, to be the one watching out. Then he remembers if his wife were here, this dinner would not be taking place at all.

He chooses a tomato, puts it into his basket.

2 ✐ Marina is relaxing in the bathtub with her feet propped up against the drain, a plastic tugboat bobbing next to her right hip. Carolina has miraculously gone down for a nap, after having wakened at four in the morning and again at five.

Marina should probably be dressing by now. Yo would pick them up in less than an hour, but she feels curiously reluctant, unwilling to take the next step into relationship, into familia. She and Carolina *are* the family, she must keep that in mind, a small family ready to leave in the night, set up somewhere else, gitanas, on the move.

She runs her tongue over the tooth that David chipped with his fist. Training to stay in touch with the ragged sharp edge that divides people, in their intent, in their ways, in their assumptions. Cuidado, she tells herself.

She runs more hot water into the tub, sinks down deep as she can. Down where she trusts Yo and her feelings for Yo. And if it were just herself, if she were new and at the be-ginning of things she could afford to be courageous in her choices and careless of how the world regarded her. She might believe then that family was not a cage but instead a bright picture she could paint herself into.

3 ✐ In the kitchen of her Airstream Yolanda mashes the back of a wooden spoon into the frijoles. The pink brown jackets on the beans split their zippers. Her eye wan-ders to the fence rail outside her kitchen window where a chameleon suns. Mash, mash, mash. The sound of Yo's spoon, the rhythm of her hand and wrist coaxing the individual beans into a blended, textured substance.

Book Two

May 9, 1983

        Aunt Josie flashes her senior citizen's annual pass
to the ticket taker and Marina follows her through the turn-
stile to the crowded Aerial Tramway waiting room.
    Marina is not sure how she came to be here. She remem-
bers Aunt Josie passing her the chicken mole at dinner Sunday and asking her if she was afraid of heights. Next thing
she knows she has somehow agreed to jam herself into a little red car with sixty tourists and ride up to the top of San
Jacinto with a woman she has just met.
    Aunt Josie's ancient Dodge Dart boiled over twice on the
way up, and both times she topped off the radiator from a
picnic jug of water she always carried in the car and just kept
on going. Everything matter of fact. Now she is sitting on the
bench embroidering a flower on the corner of a dish towel,
like she was in her own living room. Marina sits next to her
in the noisy waiting room and watches for the arrival of the
red car.
    Without looking up Aunt Josie says, "They're meeting in
the middle, right about now."
    "The middle?"
    "See, they start out at the same time," Aunt Josie explains,

looking up, scaffolding and girders reflected above the dividing line of her bifocals. It takes both hands to show it: two cars headed straight for each other, meeting in the middle, exchanging places, and going on. "It's a lot like life," says Aunt Josie. Marina waits for her to explain, but she just weaves her needle in and out, making little chains of green around a crimson flower.

Finally the car glides into the staging platform. The scene reminds Marina of a movie she saw years ago where spies hung out of funicular cars shooting at each other, then skied away across glittering snowfields. Aunt Josie guides her up next to a window, and then a recorded voice is telling them about the planning and building of the tramway and how long it is and how much it cost.

"Don't listen to any of that," says Aunt Josie, "that's just a lot a numbers the men like to talk in. All you got to do is use your eyes."

Marina looks, studies. They are moving almost straight up and she is so close to the mountain she could be a goat, one of those bighorns. She glides among rocks and outcroppings and pines growing out of sheer cliff and then patches of snow.

When their car meets its twin halfway up, there is a sudden dip in the cable that catches her heart, and a shadow falls across them that feels like doom. But after the pause they slide quickly by, free and rising, the air thinning, growing chill and clean.

"See," says Aunt Josie.

At the top they pass pink-cheeked men and women bundled in thick clothing, carrying snowshoes, heading for the car she and Aunt Josie have just vacated.

"I'd like to try them snowshoes out one day," says Aunt Josie, heading down the stairs.

At the trailhead they stop so Aunt Josie can put on her yellow sweater and Marina her green jacket. The sun is shining and the sky is brilliant blue. The air smells like scorched pine sap and there are squirrels racing around and a group of schoolchildren herded by three frazzled-looking adults. A sign says to leave only footprints, take only pictures, stay on the trails, that the world is fragile.

"I'm not going to kid you," says Aunt Josie breathing hard, "I ain't no athlete." She looks down at her square feet enclosed in white Keds. "I'm going to show you my own special place and then go right on back to the patio and buy me a hot dog. Minute I get up here I'm thinking about that hot dog. But if you got places to go by yourself, then bueno, I can wait up there on that patio all the living day for you. Got the whole world to look at and my sewing to keep me busy. Me, I don't never get bored."

Aunt Josie's trail leads past the mules blowing their lips and stomping in a ring, then up toward the ridge. The schoolchildren are headed in the opposite direction, their cries and calls echoing, then gradually fading to nothing. Now the two women hear only the dusty thump of their own feet on the trail, the cry of a red-tailed hawk, the scolding of a squirrel.

Before long, Marina's carrying both the sweater and the

jacket. Aunt Josie pauses, might be tired. Marina notices a bench made of split logs where they can rest.

They sit quietly, then Aunt Josie takes a bottle of water out of her bag and hands it to Marina. "I could say a whole lot about all of this, but I ain't going to."

"I like it here," says Marina, then drinks thirstily.

"Well, it's true you can see these mountains from a distance. Like when you're down there, in the Coachella. Whenever you look up, there they are. They're around you all the time, kind of like familia. But that's a different thing, being down there looking up, a different kind of mountain than when you're right up here with them.

"Yes, me I like it this way best and that's why I got me a senior citizen pass, so I can come up here much as I want to. You know, it's kind of nice what you get if you can just live long enough to collect it all. Discount movies, half-price dinners, bus passes.

"If I was to tell you anything at all, Marina, it might be: live a long time." She pats Marina's knee. "Now let me show you my special place."

The path curves at the rim of a cliff and then circles back toward the tramway. Aunt Josie leaves the marked trail here, following a fainter one, maybe her own, maybe just one of the many trails of various shade, route, distinction, the ones you are not supposed to take.

Marina walks a little ways behind, unexpectedly sees something glimmering under a bush. Something. She leans down quickly and wraps her hand around a warm roll of film, pictures taken, lost—never developed, studied, pasted into books—who knows how long ago. She slips the film into her jeans pocket. At first she thinks of it as trash to be thrown away (leave only footprints); then again it might be a message in a bottle (live a long time). And besides, it's how she thinks: in pictures; takes them—mentally—in the present, studies them later in her inner darkroom.

Aunt Josie pauses at the edge of a cliff, makes a sweeping gesture with her arm extended, her hand palm up, her fingers outstretched. Like she is introducing somebody. "There, mi'ja, there she is. La Coachella."

They stand side by side, looking down at the colored squares, too high up to see movement.

"Ecru, sepia, umber, Titian, russet." Marina is lost for a moment in the art of desert, then notices Aunt Josie looking at her. "Moreno," she explains, "I thought there'd be more green."

"Yeah, but Gary Luna, he used to say things wasn't always like this here in the valley. Dry, brown. His people say ten thousand years ago the whole Coachella was filled with a great lake, and around that lake there was big oak trees, plenty of green grass. Buffalo. A different kind of world then."

As Marina looks the valley fills with color. She sees the expanse of dancing waters, sees the buffalo clustered under stands of oak, sees grassland stirring in the breeze. A different world then. "What happened?" she wonders.

"Oh, you know, earthquakes, mountains coming up, rain coming down. Change. Lot of things just happening natural, like they do. But also people done it. You know, esos gabachos with their stinking yellow máquinas. Plowing things up, knocking them down, shooting them. The Corps of Engineers done a lot of it. See that Salton Sea over there?" She points east. "Just a big mistake they made. Always thinking they can move things around. Well, that one come up in the wrong place." She laughs.

"Oh we know them engineers, me and Crescencio. Him and me, we used to live in a pretty little town in Mexico. Long time ago. Here comes the Corps of Engineers saying they're going to flood the whole town. People downstream got to have water. Things got to develop. Say they know what they're doing, and we can go live someplace else. Like it's all the same. And it *is* the same, time they're through with it.

"But I'll tell you that cuento another time, Marina. Let's go get us a hot dog."

May 10, 1983

1 ✐ Because Gilberto is still in the hospital, Marina finishes up work quickly, has time to drop by the Palm Springs Pharmacy and pick up that film she dropped off last night, the film from the trail, then she'll get Carolina from Lupe's. Yesterday afternoon, coming down on the tramway, she could feel a plan wrap itself around the warm roll of film in her pocket.

Lately the closer she got to Yolanda, the more uneasy she became over the missing pieces in the story meant to replace her past. Maybe this roll of film, presented to her in such an unexpected way, held images she could cluster around herself and Carolina, lending depth and credibility to her history, family photos in frames on the wall. Cousins, aunts, nieces. Uncles bent over the engines of cars, her grandmother at the beach holding up a drumstick, laughing into the camera.

Not that she wanted to fool Yo. There was more than enough of that going on. Necessary deceptions. To keep her and Carolina safe. The two of them. Alone.

Maybe, driving to the drugstore, Marina just wants for herself the pictures of the family that life has required her to imagine. She thinks of her real mother: dead; her real father, whom she must not call. That day in February when Isabel Ochoa Dryfus became Marina Lomas, whatever was lost to her that evening might have become images on this undeveloped roll of film. Maybe somebody, something, was beginning to give back. Recompense. Compensation. For something taken, something is returned.

Her eyes remember the blaze of Kodak yellow under the bush; her thigh remembers the heat from the pocketed film. What was bright and warm must have meaning.

She pulls now into the parking lot, turns off the engine, fishes for the receipt in her purse. The receipt that she carries through the dry heat and into the air-conditioning of the drugstore is as real as the film had been. Now she will make a simple exchange, the receipt in place of the snapshots on the film that belongs to her.

Behind the counter is a woman in her late fifties with heavy makeup and a lazy eye who wears a badge saying she is there to serve but who seems really to be there for the purpose of conversing with the customer before Marina, a tourist in pink tank top, tight white pants, jeweled ballerina slippers, her hair bleached and sprayed. They are speaking in that aggrieved tone that requires mutual assent—sometimes expressed, sometimes implied—to fuel it. The clerk says the whole town is filled with those people, you know who I mean, lady boys, and the customer says but you have to admit they are certainly artistic, still, isn't it awful about this sickness they carry with them, putting everybody at risk, regular people who have never done anything to anybody, and suddenly for Marina—who has been only half listening to their conversation, to the news, to the world—indistinct images of the past two months draw into shapes she can finally read, negative becomes positive becomes negative becomes positive: Gilberto has this sickness, this plague, this AIDS. And everybody all along has known it except her. But nobody has said.

She sets down the scrap of paper on the counter, turns, and strides back out through automatic doors.

2 ✏ Yo pulls her Camaro up close behind Marina's blue wagon. Soon as the engine's off she hears Carolina. Loud. Mad, maybe. She knocks on the door, but Marina can't hear. She edges it open and calls out. A voice that doesn't really mean it yells, Come in. Something tells her not to go down the hall but to wait. She sinks down onto the thrift shop couch.

Marina backs out of Carolina's room and closes the door on the crying, but of course it comes right through anyway, and then they are both just staring at each other, Marina sitting on the edge of a breakfast nook cushion instead of beside her on the couch. They have not touched.

"You're off work early, Yolanda."

"I was in Mac's room when you called. They're very upset. I'm upset."

"He should have told me. Both of them. They should have been up front."

"They thought you knew."

"How do you think that sounds to me? Either estoy tonta, or they were lying to me. You might be thinking I'm pretty stupid too. All of you. Well, I got news for you. I know a hell of a lot more than you think I do. I know I'm better off by myself, like I was. Me and Carolina. Tenemos una vida. Maybe you don't know that . . ."

"Sí, yo lo sé," says Yo miserably.

"Mac told me Gil was sick, that's all. Nunca AIDS. He never said AIDS to me. I've got Carolina to think about. People are dying of this, Yo. Y aquí estoy, right in the middle of it all."

"¿Estás enojada conmiga? You know I never meant to . . ."

Marina gets up, walks over to the window, glances up at Yo's trailer without knowing she is doing it: de costumbre. "You knew. Tú sabías todo. You're smart, you're observant, muy curiosa; this is just the kind of thing you like to know about, read about, study, and you never told me. Watched me go off to work every damn day of the week and never said one word. Ninguna palabra."

"Let me get Carolina, OK? She's yelling her head off."

"That's a part of it, Yo. The crying part. Sometimes it's just got to happen."

"I understand that, Marina."

"I've got Carolina to think about." She is crying now herself. "Yo quiero que te vayas to your own place, Yolanda. There's nothing more you can do here. It's all done."

Yo just sits there for a minute, waits until she's good and mad herself, so she'll have the strength to get as far as the door and close it behind her.

When Yo steps into her Airstream she can see with a pure anger that she has let her life change. Get cluttered, disorganized. Invaded, routed, usurped, ousted, deposed. There's a box of disposable diapers open on the couch, a pink pacifier lying on the kitchen table, a broken teething biscuit lying on the kitchen counter with a trail of black ants moving off toward the window like an extended ellipsis: dot, dot, dot. Her plants in the window are half dead of neglect. Christ almighty!

She tosses her purse and the blue notebook onto the couch, grabs a Corona out of the fridge. No limes. Only thing in there besides the half sixpack of beer is a jell-filled teething ring with circus animals, a blue plastic nursing bottle of apple juice, and three brown eggs.

In the bedroom Yo changes into a T-shirt and cutoffs. The bed is unmade, the red candle on her side has dripped onto the nightstand like a trail of blood. When she flings the covers off to change the sheets she surprises Carolina's teddy huddled in the middle. Holy shit!

She wads up the sheets, smells Marina in the concentration of cloth: Marina, Marina, her Marina. Stuffs everything down into the laundry basket, carries it out to the car, ready for the laundromat. Get this out of the house now. Right now. Slams down the trunk. Stands in the striped shade from the ramada over her door looking off into the desert, contemplating the idea of mirage, that which shimmers in the distance, promises oasis, recedes, disappears on approach.

Damn! She wishes she had not quit smoking last year. If she had a cigarette she would smoke it right now. Just one. Lupe smokes. She sets off running toward Lupe's, in searing heat, across gravel, feeling the splash of tears, sweat forming on her upper lip. The taste of salt; salt burning her eyes. Damn, damn, damn. What is she doing?

She stops in the middle of the deserted road breathing hard. Feels herself to be standing squarely on the fault line. This is not what she wants for herself. Is she plain crazy? She wants to love the way that poet she read in college talked about: Adrienne Rich. Yo wants to love this time with her whole intelligence. But what did it mean, to love with her whole intelligence? And how could she do it?

Back at the trailer she places the blue notebook on the kitchen table, in front of her chair. Sharpens a new yellow pencil and aligns it with the notebook. Opens another Corona, and sits down. It's time to connect the dots. All of them. Has she been deliberately not connecting the dots? Putting it off? Scared, maybe?

But how to begin, where to start? She chews on the eraser, then tosses the pencil aside, hops up to get her new green pen, the one she charged on her Visa because she knew she could think better, write better with it. Okay. She pulls the cap off, snaps it onto the opposite end, and writes out the question that's on her mind, the hard, the fair one: What is Marina right about?

She swallows some beer, gazes out the window at the afternoon light on the copper hills, checks—without realizing it, de costumbre—Marina's place: the lights on, car in place. Bueno.

What is Marina right about? She takes up the pen, writing fast, whatever comes, answering the question in every way she can think of, numbering the answers, giving this her whole intelligence. What is Marina right about?

1. That she—Yo—never said AIDS. (Why? Because if you don't say it then nobody's got it? Because if your friend's got it then you're queer too? Because it's not possible to be entirely glad you're queer? Maybe that. But wait a minute: *nobody* said AIDS much. Not anybody. Ever. A little on the news. Nobody at work talking, that was for sure, aside from all those gummed warnings stuck to a few doors at the end of one hall on the seventh floor. Was she, Yolanda Ramírez, part of a professional secret?)

2. That Gil and Mac never said AIDS. (Why? Because if you could say it you were going to die of it? Because where do you go when you die; maybe nowhere; like a candle, you just went out? Because if you had AIDS you might deserve to die? Because if the straight world wasn't going to mention it then the nicest thing you could do was to shut up about it too?)

There goddamn well was a secret here; she and the whole gay community had been conscripted into keeping it. And she had been the worst. Because she knew something, had a piece of the puzzle that she had carried around for weeks in a blue notebook, not showing it to anybody, the piece that might connect AIDS right back to the hospital.

Like Crescencio always said, in the hospital they make you sick. Every single day the hospital was working to spread AIDS throughout the whole Coachella Valley, spreading it to hemophiliacs, surgery patients, body shop clients, women who thought they were old and ugly and therefore useless: refuse in a glittering world. Women like Eliana Townsend.

Yo stands up and finishes off the Corona, glances down to Marina's place. Her trailer, battered and alone like that, looked like some kind of forlorn prehistoric monster, stranded, without food or company or help.

The first place Yo had gotten off track was with Marina. Lying to her meant lying to herself, and that meant a wobble developing at the base of the whole turning world.

So tonight she would clean up her house, give Silvia Cedeño a call, maybe figure out how to get inside that secret place where those gabachos laid their plans. If she worked hard and fast and honest, got right with herself and the world, then she might get right with Marina too. In time. In time.

3 ⌀ David Dryfus is not a patient man. Waiting for a meal in a restaurant, he's inclined to tap all four fingers of his right hand in a repeated and rhythmic pattern that others find annoying. However, there is nobody present tonight at his table in Chez Pascal to object to this nervous habit. Nobody to whom he can recount his day, nobody to hear his stories, to tell her own in exchange.

He finds himself getting tired, really tired, of coming home to an empty house and eating frozen dinners in front of the television; or out alone, as now; or occasionally at friends' houses, the man with no partner. An irrational number.

He is tired of dealing with the mystery of Isabel's flight, of her present whereabouts, the mystery that has gone on too long, that has become tedious. How many times is he expected to tell people Isabel is visiting, still visiting, her father in Juárez, has an open ticket?

Against his will he has been plunged into mystery, somehow held captive in that temporal zone between the question and the answer. But if you could ask him what shape life ought to take, he would tell you this: that life should be like a map on which one could chart one's clear course. And those of others. Life should have a legend by which one could calculate distance, speed, points of intersection. Somewhere on the map it should say: YOU ARE HERE. By traveling at a certain speed, for a certain length of time, one should be able to estimate one's approximate time of arrival and the probable outcome.

May 11, 1983

When Yo comes into the hospital snack room, Silvia Cedeño is sitting back, smoking, in a Naugahyde and chrome chair, her lunch bag crumpled up on the table in front of her.

"Sorry I couldn't make it sooner," Yo says, sitting down with her green lunch pail.

"Why do I have the feeling this is going to cost me?" Silvia picks up her lunch sack and smashes it into the container behind her, pulls the ashtray closer. "Well, shoot."

Yo takes the lid off her yogurt. "Silvia, I want you to get me in to see the boss. Reed. I need to talk to him."

"Talk to me," says Silvia, lighting a cigarette with her red Bic lighter and exhaling a stream of smoke over Yo's left shoulder. "I'm your boss. Talk to me. You got five minutes."

"Well, we got a bunch of women keep checking in and out of the hospital. In and out; in and out. Seems like they can never get well. I picked out four, been reading their files: Eliana Townsend, Mina West, Tootie Greenwald, and Dorie Atwater."

"Whoa, girlfriend. You got no authorization to look at those files. They're confidential. You know that, Yolanda Ramírez."

"Look Silvia, we got ourselves a situation here. West is a hemophiliac; Townsend, Greenwald, and Atwater all been to the body shop, all been transfused. Then back they come: flu, pneumonia, hepatitis, fungal infections, you name it. The same diseases we see early on in AIDS patients."

"Hepatitis ain't AIDS, Yo, you know that." She stubs out her cigarette.

"I also know they got all the signs in their blood." She counts on her fingers: "T-cells in the basement, low macrophages, low white cells; ditto for the B-cells. Now you tell me."

"Lotta things could cause that." Silvia looks at her watch. "And you better not let Reed hear you calling his Contouring Centre the body shop."

Yo's hand goes out, she grips Silvia's wrist. "Oígame, Silvia. What if I'm right?"

Silvia withdraws her hand. "What if you're wrong? You could lose your job. You could lose *my* job. I'm fifty-five years old, niña." She shakes another cigarette out of the pack. "Besides, it doesn't make any sense. How could these ladies be coming down with AIDS?"

Yolanda lowers her voice. "What if we're giving it to them?"

"You telling me they got AIDS right here, from transfusions? No way." She snaps her lighter into flame.

"Think about it, Sil."

"We don't use transfusion systems but once. All that stuff's sterile, comes packed up tight in plastic. It's virgin."

"Okay, okay. But let's try something else. Let's say the delivery system is perfectly fine. But what about the blood it-

self, Silvia? Can you say the blood's sterile? No you can't. Because it's not heated, it's only filtered. 'Cause it's cheaper."

"Filtration's enough. It's all you need, for Christ's sake."

"But what if AIDS is a virus? Filters can't screen out viruses.
You got to cook viruses to kill them."

"If, if, if. You know how many ifs you got here, Yolanda?
Fact is nobody knows what causes AIDS, not the scientists,
not the doctors, and not even you, girlfriend. I got to get
back to work." She crumples up the empty Marlboro pack
and gets to her feet.

"Okay, but one more thing. One more." Yo pats the Naugahyde chair, coaxing her supervisor back into place. "Silvia, tell me, where does that blood come from?"

"Blood bank, most of it. People donate it. You know that."

"People, yes, but what people? Maybe they got AIDS and
don't know they got it. And what about the rest of the blood?
The blood that's bought and paid for. Where does that come
from?"

"Christ, I don't know where it comes from, Yo. I don't know
where the toilet seats come from either."

"Okay, fine. Let's talk about toilet seats. We get blood and
toilet seats the same way, from suppliers, businesses, big
businesses. Four billion a year just for plasma products. You
and I don't know where the hell they're getting all that blood
from, esos gabachos, because they don't want us to know.
But Silvia, somebody's getting rich off of this, filthy rich.
Count on it."

"And it ain't us," Silvia says, shooting a cautionary glance in the direction of an intern dropping quarters into the Coke machine, "that's for sure."

The two women sit in the silence, listening to the sound of money falling into places they can't see. Silvia gets slowly to her feet, leans close, says, "Let me see what I can do."

Late in the afternoon Yo gives a quick knock and opens Aunt Josie's front door suddenly. Her aunt, who has been re-laxing in her La-Z-Boy watching a rerun of the "Rockford Files," gives a little yip of terror, laughs, reaches up for a hug. Then she clicks off the remote, levers down her legs.

"Don't turn it off," Yo protests.

"Oh mi'ja, I seen this one already. They was about to break into his trailer. His cover was busted."

"And his dad was there fixing the plumbing?"

"That's the one. Say let's have a Modelo and maybe some chips. I got a nice avocado Crescencio brung me."

In the kitchen, Yo flips off the caps and pours her aunt's beer into a glass. Aunt Josie is peeling the avocado for gua-camole, but pauses, takes her glass, lifts it.

"I don't know exactly what we're celebrating, Yolanda, but I feel like that's what we're doing. How come I feel that? It's not about me getting the day off, because these days that means la señora is not doing good. That husband checks her into the hospital again. So it ain't me we're celebrating. It might be you."

"To Silvia Cedeño," says Yo, touching her aunt's glass with her brown bottle. "Una mujer grande y fuerte."

"I think you got a story here, mi'ja. Get those chips out of the cupboard while I finish up with the guacamole. Put everything out where we can get it good; on the coffee table."

In a few minutes they're settled. Yo tells Tía Josie about the blood and that Silvia has agreed to get her in to see Reed. Aunt Josie has been listening carefully, and now she sits thinking. Yo runs a chip through the guacamole, crunches, waits.

"It's this," says Aunt Josie. "I'm thinking about la señora now. You telling me this lady's got AIDS. I know all about this sickness from the Dan Rather, so I know what you're saying to me. And you're saying she got it from the blood."

Yo nods. "Exactamente."

"And you're telling me this lady's not going to hear it from the gabacho doctors because they got to keep on looking like they're perfect?"

Yo nods again.

"Then," says Aunt Josie, "we got to tell her ourselves. 'Cause she's real upset, that lady, all the time. They been telling her she's loca, esos doctores. Tú lo sabes."

"Aunt Josie," says Yo, "you know how Rockford never lets on what he knows until just the right minute? Timing I'm talking about. The timing's got to be just right."

"So don't tell her, you're saying?"

Yo shakes her head. "Ahora, no. It wouldn't be fair to her either. Not till I know more. I got to be sure. Talk to Reed. Get things in place, ¿me entiendes?

Aunt Josie drinks solemnly from her glass. "I don't keep nothing from Crescencio. Nunca."

"Just make sure he understands that we've all got to wait. The time is coming. Tell him the time is coming around. I'm working on it."

"I know you are, mi'ja. And it must be hard llevando toda esa información around inside of yourself, all those secrets. ¡Dios mío! You told Marina about all this? I like that Marina. You can tell her things."

They sit, the window unit stirring air around them, filling up the silence. "What?" asks Josie. "¿Qué tienes? You mad at her?"

"She's mad at me."

"Get yourself otra cerveza. You need it. Love trouble's the worst kind of trouble there is. Get me one too."

Yo gets up, pauses at the front window, watches for a moment the cottonwoods flickering in the warm afternoon breeze, playing with light. From the kitchen she calls to her aunt, "These are the last two." She comes back into the living room holding aloft the two dark bottles, pours one into her aunt's empty glass.

"I been thinking about Gary Luna all day long," Aunt Josie says. "Whenever I put on these old house shoes of his I think about him." She looks down at her feet with curiosity.

"What does Tío think I should do?"

She laughs, drinks from her light-filled glass. "What does he know? I'm telling you, talk it over. What else you going to do? Here you are, walking around with all those big

secrets inside of you, ones you got to keep. Don't get confused about what to hold, what to let go. That's what I say."

Yo drinks from the brown bottle, looks at her watch. "It's
six o'clock, Tía."

"Oh thanks, mi'ja, the Dan Rather." She clicks on her remote, changes channels. "I wish they'd bring back that nice
Walter Cronkite on the TV. Seems like we was all a lot better off when he was keeping an eye on things." She mutes
the sound while the loud, bright commercials spin.

"Y ese Ronald Reagan," says Yo, sinking deep into the ancient aqua couch.

"Yeah," says her aunt, "that one. He's the problem. I never
did like his movies."

"I can't even watch the news anymore. Too depressing."

"Oh you got to watch it, mi'ja. How else you going to know
what the gabachos are going to do next? Keep your eye on
them is what I say. You stop paying attention and those men
in suits will carry off everything that's not nailed down."

She struggles up out of the sunken part of the couch and
switches off the air conditioner, opens the front door, then
the windows, one by one, letting in the song of cricket and
bird. "Ah, that's better. Lows in the mid-fifties, they're saying."

Yo can hear the cottonwoods now, like a running river,
like a secret being told.

Biscuit Reed always takes her time getting her belongings out of the back seat of her car Sunday afternoons just before she goes into the Coachella Public Library. There's a little rose-colored frame house across the street from her parking place that she enjoys glancing into, casually, so they don't notice. And really she is not being judgmental. She likes the little house, the cheerful color of it, the way all the friends and family park right there in the front yard just any old way, and how music and laughter come spilling out the windows and doors heedless as sunlight.

It might be fun to be Mexican and have all those people with no work ethic just hanging around with you on Sundays and eating all kinds of spicy, fattening food together like there's no tomorrow. What if she just strolled across the road right now and picked her way up the broken concrete walk to the front door of the pink house with turquoise trim?

But her feet keep her going the right way, up the walk toward the library, carrying under one arm the Sunday paper and under the other the book on golf she checked out for Harold last week. Thinking about the pink house keeps Biscuit from noticing the woman waiting by the front door until she is right up on her. The drug addict. That wild-eyed Mexican woman doing research on AIDS.

Well Biscuit has the medical journal she ordered through interlibrary loan, and one or two more of the books she wanted. That ought to hold her. Biscuit keeps wanting to ask her in a nice tone of voice if she's a doctor, but that might be passive-aggressive and Biscuit does not want to be that ever, watches herself for signs of it.

So she smiles at the woman while unlocking the front door and tells her she has her materials if she will just give her a few minutes to get organized. The woman goes off to the far side of the library and paces up and down, snapping her fingers and popping her knuckles every now and then, a habit Biscuit can barely tolerate even in men.

Then suddenly this woman is looming over Biscuit at the check-out desk; she has waited, apparently, as long as she can; flames are about to leap out of her eyes. Biscuit quickly assembles the stack of material, and the woman carries it off to the back of the library like it is game she has hunted down and will now devour in solitude. At least now it's quiet.

Biscuit breathes a sigh of relief and spreads the Sunday paper out on the desk in front of her. She and Harold always used to read the paper together every Sunday, but this new job of his requires him to play golf all the time with Mr. Disenhouse from the hospital and other influential men from the community. Sometimes movie stars. But since she and Harold cannot be together Sundays anymore she might as well be providing a service to the community. Just as he is. They are a team, in that respect. They like to give back.

She picks up the "Living" section, her favorite part of the *Desert Sun*. She'll find out who is giving parties, who is taking cruises, and who is getting married. Sometimes too she cuts out wonderful recipes and ideas for menus that help spark up their home life together.

Here for example on the front page of "Living" is a full-page layout on last week's benefit for the McCallum Theatre. She had been at that event herself, in her little black jersey with the beaded collar, though she does not see herself in any of the photos. But the week before there had been a picture of Harold playing golf in the Trini López Celebrity Golf tournament and another of them both, dancing at the fabulous Black-Tie Dinner afterward.

She turns the page. Here's a fabulous menu now, all set out like for a formal dinner, maybe with ideas she can try out in her own life. It reads:

Baked Chevre with Tomatoes and Garlic Toasts
Cream of Fennel Soup
Breasts of Chicken Stuffed with Spinach and Ginger
Oven Fried Parmesan Potatoes
Buttered Baby Carrots
Lemon Mousse
Liposuction
Abdominoplasty
Body Contouring

She has been tricked by this false menu. Tears spring to her eyes. Tricked by her own newspaper. Looking for information, she has been judged and found wanting. Guilty as charged. For right this moment did not a two-pound box of Mrs. See's finest candies nestle in the bottom drawer of her dressing table? She can see it magnified a thousand times, the box of chocolates, floating over the Recent Acquisitions table.

Biscuit's heart pounds and she feels the rising tide of a hot flash. She will imagine, as her stress management tape suggests, that she is on a surfboard in Hawaii—she never knows whether to sit or stand—and riding the crest of a giant blue wave until it washes up on the beach of well-being.

There. Now she has the composure to understand and to make rational judgments. This ad for the Contouring Centre might be, come to think of it, a sign. Things do come to her in this way. It could be a reminder of something she really needs to do. Weeks ago she made up her mind to get that facial rejuvenation done and never had called to make the appointment. She is exactly the kind of person who wanders down the menu of life little considering the eventual cost. This message must have been written for her.

There is also Harold's position to consider. His duties include overseeing the work of the Contouring Centre. It would not be fair to Harold to just let herself go, when he himself was dedicating his life to helping women stay beautiful and desirable.

She is reaching for the phone to schedule an appointment

when the library door flies open and here comes that other woman, the one with the plum hair who likes to read the obituaries so much. But people will surprise you; instead she asks for books on AIDS. This thing is spreading, it looks like.

While Biscuit is reaching under the counter to get what's left of them, the first woman, the aggressive one at the back of the room, jumps up and comes over, hugs this woman with the purple hair, and then they are talking fast in Spanish and carrying the two books from under the counter over to the others heaped up on the back table where they now sit taking notes, whispering, grinning, and looking at each other like long lost sisters.

Biscuit searches through the list under Surgery—Plastic in the Yellow Pages, picks up the receiver, and punches in the phone number of the Contouring Centre. Then she remembers it is, after all, Sunday. She'll call tomorrow morning. First thing.

May 15, 1983

1 ✐ Harold Eden Reed looks up from the expanse of his desk and sees Yolanda Ramírez standing before him in a white lab coat. She is neat, almost pretty, but her hair's too short and her earrings too large. Harold has noticed many of the Hispanic women on his staff wearing earrings too large, suggesting a certain lack of taste. The shadow along her upper lip will probably become, in middle age, a moustache.

He beckons, and she sits down rather too comfortably in the chair in front of his desk. "Mr. Reed," she says, "I'm Yolanda Ramírez, a phlebotomist on the laboratory staff."

"Yes," he says, "I was told you wished to see me, Miss Ramírez."

"I appreciate you taking the time. I've been doing some reading, research really, that I'd like to talk with you about."

"Research?"

"About the AIDS epidemic."

"Well," he says, smiling, "I really think *epidemic* is too strong a word. Don't you?"

"There are more than a thousand cases to date, sir."

"Miss Ramírez, you can rest assured that the medical staff and I are keeping an eye on this developing situation. We're on top of things. And bear in mind, too, that these incidents are falling within a highly restricted segment of the general population. Highly restricted."

"But many are also falling *outside* this highly restricted segment."

"I include Haitian drug addicts."

"I'm thinking about the hemophiliacs, Mr. Reed. Several have come down with AIDS. We've got one in the hospital right now. These people are not gay, not IV drug users, just plain hemophiliacs and they're showing up with AIDS. I've read that this fact alone proves AIDS can be transmitted through blood transfusion. And if that's right, then anybody can get it. That's the point that I thought might really interest you."

Harold Reed keeps his eyes on his orderly desk, places the letter opener at the top of his blotter, looks up when his employee finishes speaking, says, "Are you training to be a doctor, Miss Ramírez?"

"Mr. Reed, these are facts anybody can come by. In the library, even in some of the newspapers. It's true nobody seems to be paying much attention, but the facts are there. That article in the *New York Times* last winter . . ."

"I wonder if you couldn't invest just a little trust and confidence in men infinitely more qualified than you to alert this community in the event of real danger. I hardly think this hospital should cease to function because a lab technician with an AA degree from the local junior college says the blood supply is tainted."

This has clearly slowed her down. It takes her a minute to recover, to go on with her allegations.

"I'm not saying the blood's tainted. I haven't said that. But consider the facts. If the virus can be carried in the blood—"

"But Miss Ramírez, we do not know that it even *is* a virus."

"Say that it is, sir, and—"

"I am not going to permit you to dictate to me—"

"I am not dictating; I am suggesting. I am suggesting that we scrutinize the sources of our blood and that until we know more we could kind of slow down with the surgeries, cut out elective surgery, at least."

"Are you suggesting this hospital performs unnecessary surgeries, Miss Ramírez? Because if you are . . ."

"No sir. Of course not. But we just might take a second look where surgery could be postponed. Maybe get a second opinion for women scheduled for hysterectomy. Delay surgeries temporarily at the Contouring Centre."

"Clients of our Contouring Centre might not agree with you that their surgery constitutes a medical frivolity, Miss Ramírez. In our society—though this may come as a surprise to you—beauty is highly prized, not just by men but by women themselves. A woman's self-esteem depends upon it. Take a women with insignificant breasts who has suffered her whole life from this defect. Consider the woman who has lost an essential part of herself to the ravages of cancer. She loses her femininity, her power to attract. What about the husband of this woman?

"No, Miss Ramírez, these are desperate women whose feelings must be considered and even protected. And you know very well as a professional that transfusion is seldom required among our contouring clients."

"Liposuction patients often need it. Same with breast reduction. Complications happen. If a woman's got high blood pressure, or is a little slow to clot . . ."

Harold Reed is standing, opening and closing drawers in his desk, tossing folders into his briefcase. Then he looks down at this lab technician and says, "Let me share with you something from my personal life, Miss Ramírez, and then you really must excuse me; I have a meeting shortly. My own wife, whom you may well know as one of our candy stripers, Biscuit Reed, has just made an appointment for a blepharoplasty at our Contouring Centre. If there were even the slightest risk in this procedure, do you honestly believe I would permit it?"

2 ⌀ Crescencio looks up from his work when he hears the van pull up. From behind the branches of a grapefruit tree he watches the joven go to the Townsends' door with the oxygen tanks. La señora, again, and this time maybe he knows what's going on, why she's sick. He won't say anything, though. Not without proof. Too many people already telling her what's what. He's just going to stay close by, kind of keep an eye on things, see what happens. His daughter says the time is coming around.

Crescencio is tilling lightly around the grapefruit trees with the special tool he made for himself when he was a joven in Guerrero before he and Josefina had been forced to leave their beautiful town—what?—thirty years ago. Thirty years. A long time. A lifetime.

In his mind he has been searching back, trying to find the point when the world made a strange turn in the wrong direction, one that led like a path straight to the front door of la señora, where air arrived in tanks carried by strangers. And now, maybe he has found it, the starting point. Found it by the feel of his hand on the wood of the implement he made thirty years ago in Guerrero Viejo.

Viejo because now there was a new town, Nuevo Guerrero, built out of ugly cinder block, thirty-six miles away from the real Guerrero, his own town covered over now by water those government men dammed up, men in suits, ties, dark glasses you could see yourself in but not their eyes. Dammed up the whole Río Grande. ¿Y por qué? Why did esos gabachos—¿cómo se dicen? this Corps of Engineers—decide to flood his beautiful town, to drown the alameda, the mercado, la catedrál, his school, the house he was born in? Why? Why did they do this?

To bring water to the ugly towns springing up all along the Tamaulipas border, to bring it to the farmers downriver so they could get rich, and the new money would bring más dinero y más y más.

People didn't understand what growing meant anymore, like it was just sticking one thing on top another, the kind of growing that turned into cancer. Go ahead, call it cancer, because that's what it was. New Guerrero. He stopped, took off his hat, mopped his brow, began again the meditative motion, digging into the soil with the blade of his memory.

He should of stayed there, beside the old town. Some people had. He thought about Julia Zamora. Julia. She moved, all right, to the new town when they told her to. But she didn't like it. Too ugly, she said. She wanted her beautiful town back, two hundred years old; she wanted to see the arches of the mercado; wanted to stand under the high sloping roof of the catedrál; to hear again the crack of the baseball bat after school; to whirl about to melodies from the Hotel Flores's piano and the bands in the alameda on Sundays.

She went back, that Julia Zamora. Lives there now in a little house by the lake with no electricity, only ice and candles. Sells fish and soda pop to tourists. Her boat floats over the school, circles the plaza. She drops her fishing line down into his back yard. In a letter she wrote: People are returning all the time. More than twenty. Come back, Crescencio, you can live this way.

But he was married by then, had a baby. His wife told him, "It's gone, Crescencio. You got to live in this world now."

Sometimes at night he dreams he is standing again with the people of Guerrero watching the river rising. He can hear the strange music of their weeping, their cries mingling with the sound of rushing river water, can feel the chill climbing his body, until he wakes, shaking with cold, sobbing for air.

3 ✐ David is awake again in his house in Des Moines, the house to which his wife does not return. He is

listening to spring rains pelt his house and whip his windows.

He thinks of rain in Mexico, remembers running along the upper balcony late at night from his room down to Isabel's, in her parents' house.

He stands in the doorway of her bedroom, wind gusting around him, pajamas clinging to his legs, the room illuminated by flashes of lightning.

She is there, breathing like the storm. "David," she says, "David, come to me."

4 ✐ Four men alight from a golf cart and make their way toward the sixteenth hole across the thick, verdant turf that Jaime Luna, in his big green tank truck, sprayed thoroughly the evening before with a mixture of fertilizer and Diazinon.

Harold Eden Reed has been struggling for sixteen holes to bring up the question of the blood supply. He watches his superior, Meredith Disenhouse, address the ball. Harold holds his breath, out of respect.

The provost from the College of the Desert is dressed in turquoise slacks and a cream-colored golf shirt that says C.O.D. in matching turquoise over his heart. He brings to the game a certain air of gravity that is quite lost on the other man, Ralph Sooner, who is younger than the other three and is inclined to chat while they're playing. Disenhouse had to speak to him about it on the tenth hole, when his patience ran out. But Sooner, a developer new to the Coachella Valley, must be thinking of contributing to the hospital or he would not be here. Disenhouse does not confide in Reed about such matters.

Harold Reed is lucky to have this job as executive vice-president. He is not getting any younger, was out of work for almost a year when he lost his position at Orlando Memorial during restructuring. Besides, Palm Springs has welcomed the Reeds. Offered them shelter. They have a lovely home, belong to this country club, the Shriners, the Chamber of Commerce. In return they volunteer, serve the community, give back. They plan one day to retire here in this oasis of nature and culture.

Mr. Disenhouse has placed his ball within range of the cup and smiles ever so faintly as he slides his three iron back into the bag. Now he watches with exaggerated interest as Sooner lines up his shot. A good time, Harold thinks, to bring up this matter of the blood.

"You know, Meri," he begins tentatively, underplaying the use of the nickname because sometimes Disenhouse likes to be addressed as Meri and sometimes not, "I've been hearing some rumors about the blood supply."

No response. Sooner looks up from where he is crouched to lodge a silent complaint. The provost, on the other hand, registers a flicker of interest.

Perhaps Harold should simply drop it. Then he finds in his confusion, perhaps out of some sense of urgency, he has said the word right out loud: AIDS. Disenhouse is staring at him, little red thermometers rising along either side of his throat. Sooner hits the ball far right of the cup, glances in irritation at Reed. The provost is examining his clubs with studied intensity.

Now Disenhouse has thrown an arm around his shoulders and is guiding him off to the side, speaking in confidential tones under a eucalyptus. "Harold, my man, what's all this about? Listening to rumors is what the wives do. This business of the blood supply is all blown out of proportion. Way out of proportion. Trust me."

Harold takes out his clean, folded handkerchief and dabs at his brow. "I've just been reading that article in the New England *Journal of Medicine*. The one on transfusions in hemophiliacs."

"I know what you're talking about, of course I know about it. You can believe I'm on top of things. That's my job. Staying in touch with my doctors, and you can bet my doctors keep me informed, up to date, in the know. Depend on it. The truth is that a lot of gossip mongers and bleeding-heart liberals are getting all worked up over nothing."

"Nothing?" says Harold. The provost is staring at his ball as if it could be moved by kinetic energy.

"Harold, now listen to me. My business is to manage the doctors; your business is to manage the community. And it's a fine community. Fine. Your job is to see to it that lay people don't get panicked by a lot of silly rumors. Do you realize what could happen in this community if people thought the blood supply was at risk? We can't allow public hysteria over this issue, Harold. That wouldn't be professional, now would it? Like yelling fire in a crowded theater. You know the sort of thing.

"And besides there's the practical side too, the business side. And we can't afford to forget that, can we? You and I are men of the world. We have responsibilities. Now what about that inventory of blood we've got on hand right now? Think about it, the size of it. What are we supposed to do with that? Say to the board, oh very sorry, we seem to have made a mistake. We couldn't *give* that plasma away once word got out. I'm not telling you anything you don't already know, Harold. You're a savvy kind of a guy. That's why I picked you as my number two man." He watches the provost's ball roll up toward the apron, then roll backwards.

"Besides," continues Meri, looking up at the provost and nodding encouragement, "there's no hard evidence on any of this. Take a look at that editorial in the last issue of *Lancet,*" he says, letting his arm drop. "Matter of fact I'll get my girl to Xerox it for you. Send it over. Right there in the April issue. A real eye-opener. Says straight out there's absolutely no proof AIDS germs can even get into blood, let alone be spread that way. These are doctors saying this. You and I, Harold, are not doctors. Are we? We're businessmen. We will just have to accept their informed opinions. Am I right or am I right?"

Harold laughs, feels a rivulet of sweat slip down his spine.

"Absolutely nothing to worry about." Disenhouse has begun studying his next shot. One more should do it. But he'll have to wait; it's Harold's turn now. The provost, whose ball has returned to the spot from which it began, stands staring morosely in the direction of Mount Jacinto.

Harold's face and arms feel tight. As he studies his clubs trying to make the right selection, he is telling himself to relax. He thinks of Biscuit and her guided imagery tapes, how she lies on the deep piled rug of their living room dressed in pink Spandex, letting a soothing male voice walk her down a beach in Hawaii.

But it doesn't work for Harold. He strikes the ball up high into an irrelevant arc, watches as it drifts down, down, falling finally into a dry wash, where it disappears into sand.

5 ✐ Meri Disenhouse feels fit after the morning's exercise. Having showered and lunched at the clubhouse he is now ready for business. His Day-Timer is open on his desk, right where he likes it. Mina takes good care of him. He calls her in and tells her to make a copy of the *Lancet* article for Reed. While he dictates an accompanying memo his experienced eye travels its customary path down Mina's legs, an activity always pleasurable in the past. Today, however, he notices an ugly sore on her left leg, something she should really cover with makeup. Unsightly.

He averts his gaze to the courtyard outside his office window: into sunshine, rich green foliage, a playing fountain. To nature.

Without looking at Mina, he begins. "To Harold Reed, re: our recent conversation concerning this community's blood supply. To more effectively utilize your talents and address your interests I am appointing you to replace me on the Blood Bank board of directors, effective immediately. Meredith Disenhouse, Hospital Administrator."

"Oh and Mina," he adds, keeping his eyes on the play of water, "please cc that to Eugene over at the Blood Bank."

After his girl leaves he gets his lawyer on the phone and tells him to have all his stock in Colter Laboratories put in his wife's name. Better safe than sorry. Besides, this is a nice little gesture to commemorate their twenty-fifth anniversary this month. Let her know she's really appreciated.

May 20, 1983

1 🖉 Biscuit Reed is resting quietly on the gur-
ney. They have given her a large blue pill. There is a drip in
her arm, but that does not trouble her. She is perfectly calm.

She is calm when the young man in green comes for her,
wheeling her off somewhere down the hall. They put her
first in a large room with other people lying under sheets,
people with liquid dripping into their arms. She has seen a
movie that looks like this but cannot remember its name or
who was in it.

She is not sure how long she has been waiting here when
Dr. Innis comes up and asks her how are we doing, and then
Dr. Jordan, her anesthesiologist. She knows them by their
eyes. Otherwise you might think they were bandits, the way
their mouths are covered.

Biscuit knows exactly what to expect. Dr. Innis has explained everything in advance. They will need her help during this little procedure. Nothing to fear because these men
are the best in the business. Harold has said so. They will
look out for her in special ways because of Harold and who
he is. His position in this hospital.

She begins to feel as if her arms are going to roll off the

sides of the narrow gurney, but just then another man in green tells her to fasten her seat belt, and then she is moving again, gliding toward a room with bright lights where she must help them move her far-off body onto the operating table.

She must help them in everything because if her eyes fall shut during the procedure then Dr. Innis cannot make the slim, unnoticeable cuts over and under her eyes and slip out the pouches of fat that time and her own carelessness have deposited there.

She will lie here quietly on this table, holding her eyes open and playing inside her mind the relaxation tape that tells her she is on the beach in Hawaii while really she is here, in this operating room. She will hold her eyes open wide, but she will see nothing. Not even the knife, when it comes for her.

2 ✐ Marina has been watching a rerun of "Perry Mason" on the television and folding diapers when the phone rings. The voice says, "Isabel?" The moment shaves itself into transparent seconds in which she is trying to remember this name and the voice that speaks it, to link back together what has been split.

"Isabel. Don't hang up. I just want to know how you are. How Caroline is."

"We're fine, David," she says, her voice echoing inside her head: David, David, David. Bad connection.

"Isabel, I want to come and see you."

"That's not possible."

"I was thinking the other night," he says, as if he has all the time in the world, as if she is a fish that his strong, taut voice can simply reel in, "about Mexico, before we got married. You remember." He waits for her to remember, plays out the line.

"Where are you?" she says.

"I'm at home, in our room. I'm sitting on our bed, Isabel." In the pause, Isabel holds herself motionless. As if she is dead. "But I'll be in LA in a week or so," he continues, "on business. I want to come down there, when I finish up. I want to see you and Caroline. We can talk. We need that. I'll come down and we'll have dinner together. Someplace nice."

"No," she says, "don't do that. Don't come here."

"I miss you," he says. "I need you. You know that. And you need me, whatever you say. I'll be coming down. When I finish up in LA."

"I'm telling you, David."

"I know where you are," he says.

Isabel hangs up the phone.

On "Perry Mason" it is becoming increasingly clear which of the characters will be the murder victim. The murderer, on the other hand, could be almost anyone.

3 ✎ What little grass there is between Yo's trailer and Marina's has been beaten completely flat in the last week. Yo likes the looks of it, likes to come home and see Marina heading up to her place with Carolina clinging to her like a monkey baby. Sometimes Yo makes dinner at her house and

carries it down the slope to Marina's. They don't plan this; it's just been happening, ever since that day in the library.

Yo is trying for now to keep all the lines of communication open and not expect too much back, although sure, she'd like to know everything, the way you can when you read a novel, the way you get to know the different characters' histories and motives and fears. Neat. Not like life.

But her life is about to get neat in a fundamental way, once she changes out of her work clothes and starts making dinner.

It was definitely not neat this afternoon when Silvia Cedeño told her to back off, that the CDC had called Harold Reed to complain about Yo's "hounding" them for information. Definitely not neat then.

But very soon Marina is going to walk up the path with Carolina riding her right hip, and three cans of beer dangling from a plastic holder in her left hand. Marina is going to come up that path already knowing the time has come to tell her story to the person she trusts most in the world.

It's like this. Imagine that she still has that roll of film she found on the mountain, that she developed it herself in her own bathroom, that the scenes on the film represent the actual scenes of her real life, and that Yo will study them with tenderness and appreciation.

Let the mysteries begin their own solutions.

May 21, 1983

It's nearly seven when Yo finally makes it to the courtyard of the Casa Diva. A few bronzed and bulging bodies recline on lounge chairs pulled up into the last remaining triangle of afternoon sunlight. Gil is parked in the shade of a palm, the wheels of his chair extending out over the pool. He smiles at her. The air is impregnated with coconut oil and chlorine.

"Don't do it, Gil," she shrieks, pulling him away from the edge.

He laughs. "Am I glad to see you, hermanita. How are you?" He yields himself to extravagant hugs and kisses. "You sounded funny on the phone. Quite fraught. Or is it wrought? You okay?"

"Let's have a drink."

"Always a good plan of action. Besides it's beastly hot out here. Roll me please, Miss Scarlet. A lethargy has quite overtaken me."

Mac is grilling on their private patio, a fan stirring the mesquite cloud encircling his head.

"Christ, that smells good," says Yo. "I could eat a cow."

"Exactly," says Mac, rising to kiss her. "Every time I make up my mind to be a vegetarian I immediately want a steak.

Keep your eye on these and I'll whiz us up some strawberry daiquiris."

"Queen!" says Gil. "Real women don't drink strawberry daiquiris."

"What do they drink?"

"Scotch and water, don't they Yo?"

"Not this real woman," says Yo, taking the tongs from Mac.

"I'd like a pink squirrel," says Gil.

"You *are* a pink squirrel," says Mac, and goes inside.

"How've you been feeling?" asks Yo, pulling a patio chair up to the grill.

"Oh better, tired, I suppose. It's nice the season's almost over and things are starting to quiet down a little. Easier on Mac, too. And Marina."

"Has Marina talked with you?"

"About what?"

"That's what I thought. It looks like she's going to need some help."

"Carolina's not—"

"No, she's fine."

"Who's fine?" asks Mac, emerging with a tray of bright drinks.

"Oh," says Gil, "they look like pink jewelry. Which one's the virgin?"

"Yours is the one with the straw. But what are we doing, children? It's too hot out here. Yo, grab the drinks." He wheels Gil through French doors and into an arched dining room. "We'll eat inside. I'll just dash back and forth. Won't take long."

"Small portions for me or I'll get depressed," says Gil.

Soon they are settled before plates of steak, grilled zucchini and corn, a mountainous Caesar salad.

"This doesn't look like a child's portion to me."

"Just eat what you want," Mac tells Gil.

"Yo needs to talk," says Gil.

"I've been wondering why you brought me here," says Mac.

"Something about Marina, I think," says Gil, buttering his corn.

"Last night she came over. After work," says Yo.

"I'm going to blush."

"Hush, Gil. Let Yo talk."

"Well, one of our problems is—"

"Now I know how Miss Manners feels."

"Gil!"

"Well, damn," says Yo, "we really don't have any problems."

"Go on. Tell Miss Manners. I'll shut up."

"It's about her life before she came here," continues Yo, sawing on her steak. "Like all I knew—or thought I knew—was she was born in Salton Sea Beach, later moved to Tucson. End of file."

"That's more than I knew."

"Let her finish," Mac says.

"So finally, last night, out it comes: she's married."

"Jumping Jesus," says Gil. "To a man?"

"Some big-shot businessman from Des Moines. She met him a long time ago in Mexico. When she was just a kid. He was a friend of her parents. Prince Charming kind of a thing, I guess."

"So they're not divorced?" asks Mac, helping himself to more salad.

"She wanted to," Yo says. "He hits her. Hits her and then of course he's sorry and he's never going to do it again and for a while he doesn't. Then he does and then he doesn't. Then they need a baby to fix the marriage and he starts in worse than before. They can work it out, he says. No divorce. Says he'll take her to court first. Get custody of Carolina."

"Could he do that?" asks Gil.

"I don't know. That's what she's afraid of. She's looking for a lawyer. I guess running off with Carolina could really count against her."

"Let's face it, being queer could count against her," says Mac. "Big time."

"That's a hell of a thing," says Gil. "What ever happened to mother's right? All this business about taking babies from their mothers just burns the hell out of me. Seems like an epidemic of it lately."

"Why did all this come up now? Does he know where she is?" Mac asks.

"He called—she doesn't know how he got her number; must have hired a PI—said he was flying to LA on business." Yo lays down her corn. "And that he's coming to see her. In a week or so. Said he knows where she is."

"She needs to get out of there, and quick. Someplace he wouldn't think to look. Gil, is anybody leaving town? Didn't Leonard Lowe say he was going to Aspen for a couple of weeks?"

"I think so," says Gil. "You know, Yolanda, you might also give Sal a call. He's a lawyer."

"I'm going to call Len about his house right now." Mac heads for the kitchen phone.

Yo turns to Gil and asks, "Why Sal?"

"He's not just a bingo lawyer, Yo. He's really good. Knows a lot of people. Has connections." Gil lays his knife and fork across his plate. "That's all I can do." He folds his napkin, then rolls his chair back a little, stretches slender arms. "But maybe we ought to just put out a contract on the husband. I don't suppose they'd take MasterCard, would they? But listen, we could do it ourselves, cheap," he says brightening. "I know we could. We're inventive, tasteful. Well, leave it at inventive. What do you think, Yo?"

"What?" says Yo, lost in thought.

"You know, rub him out. The husband."

"Make it look like an accident?"

"In my novel," says Gil, "the man with AIDS is the murderer. He commits the crime wearing a darling little tulle gown, possibly mauve. You know, just the subtlest scattering of rhinestones at the waist. Then in the middle of the night he drives the body—taking precautions to keep blood off the leather seats—in his white Lincoln Town Car to the third tee at the Dinah Shore Open and leaves him there with two nine irons crossed on his chest and an enigmatic smile on his face. Fade to black.

"Now the beauty of this plan is that even if they do identify him as the killer—which is extremely unlikely considering the man with AIDS has absolutely no motive, unless you believe that getting to wear the dear little tulle gown is motive enough—they can't really punish him. Because the man with AIDS is already dead."

"Don't be ghoulish. Besides, you can't stand the sight of blood," Yo reminds him.

"That's true," says Mac, coming back into the dining room. "You can't. How about poison?"

"Did you get Leonard?" Gil asks.

"It's all set. He leaves tomorrow afternoon and is simply thrilled to have dog sitters for the girls. They abhor staying at the vet's. Naturally. You can go by tomorrow after work and he'll give you the keys."

"And instructions," says Gil rolling his eyes. "Len is very big on instructions. Very big."

"Well," says Mac, laying his knife and fork across the plate, "they're his babies, after all. We all want the best for our babies. Don't we?"

1 ✐ George Townsend turns the key in the ignition of his Chrysler Imperial, feels the engine lunge against the parking brake, releases it, backs out of his office parking place. Stale air blows into his face, until the compressor begins to cope, cool things down. Time to go home, see Ellie. He called at noon, and she was not doing well. He spoke to the nurse. They both agreed, had agreed for almost a week, that she belonged in the hospital. But Ellie said no, they would kill her in the hospital. And Josefina said she was fine where she was, stubborn as her brother. Steady in their insisting, all three of them.

Sometimes he feels he is watching her go down, his wife. Sometimes after work instead of bearing south on Ramon Road he wants to get on I-10 driving fast, never mind where to, sights flashing by the windows like when he was candy boy on the railroad, the wheels turning and cars swaying and engine throbbing, getting him out of here and someplace safe.

No good thinking that way, though. He's faithful as a dog. Will stick it out. See her through. But Christ, it's hard. He smacks both hands on the steering wheel and gulps down a howl. She is drifting. He is losing her. One day he will sit alone in an unlit kitchen.

2 ⌀ Eliana lies alone in her darkened bedroom pretending to sleep, her thoughts moving slow and transparent as the oxygen through the plastic tubing. Her daughters are arriving next week, Ellen from Massachusetts, Andrea from Hawaii. She has asked them to stay only three or four days and then to leave. Her heart is full, uncomplicated for them. They have their own lives, and it is part of her pride that they do. They had never been for her a way of filling out her own life. And yet in her thinking, whenever she comes to this point, she stops in wonder.

Her own life. Not until this illness had she seemed to have a particular life. Her birth mother left her when she was five, traveled on with the pickers as if she did not exist. Had made no provisions. Left Eliana bewildered, to be taken in reluctantly by the widowed owner of the farm. Mothered reluctantly. Working for her keep, while the two sons had been born into rights. The right to neglect their mother. The right to leave Eliana to care for their mother in her last illness, to sit by the bed of the dying woman, claiming at the last moment the rights of the daughter.

Then she had married George, himself motherless, a young man whose gratitude had sometimes been more than she could bear. Whose anger would sometimes flame out against the children. Once she came upon him with his arm raised against Ellen. Eliana had spoken his name, watched his arm drop to his side as he remembered perhaps his own father's hand raised against him. At night, alone together, he would tell her that without her faith in him he would have been nothing. Nothing. And if it was true that her task in life had been the making of him, then what was there of her that would remain?

She thinks of her daughters, that they carry inside themselves whatever of her there is, or has been. That they carry also her mother, that brown perplexed girl of sixteen, who had moved on in her pain and misery to other fields. (Where was she now?) She thinks of the baby waiting inside her Andrea, waiting for a new story to unfold. (A grandchild!)

She will see them and they will move on, her daughters.

Her hand closes around the remote, as if she will flick on the television, as she so often does these days, but she is only trying to see, as if the future is a game show she can tune in. She sees the man child wandering in a dry land. Where is the woman who will take him in?

But having phrased this question, having struggled to shape it, she finds she knows the answer: his need will create the woman. She will come to him dressed in Eliana's clothes, her hands outstretched. He is pregnant with wives, each of them somehow her sister.

3 ✎ Yo rings Leonard Lowe's doorbell, which chimes out, "They're writing songs of love but not for me." She and Marina wait with Carolina on the porch. In a mo-

ment Len appears with a small golden poodle on his arm, like a corsage, and invites them all into his house. Yo introduces Marina and the baby. Leonard introduces Harlow, who sets up a yapping that makes Yo's ears pop.

"Harlow," says Leonard, "they'll think mama never taught you the least manners." Carolina reaches out, tangles her fingers in the curly blond topknot.

Marina extricates the dog, and Yo goes for their things. They brought both cars stuffed with their belongings. Marina has been worrying that they wouldn't be able to get out before David arrived, and to tell the truth Yo feels a little relieved now herself. She opens the trunk of her car and lifts out two large suitcases, begins stacking things up on Len's front porch.

She feels like a refugee swimming to shore with her family, and that Leonard Lowe is the Statue of Liberty. She laughs. Leonard would like that one. She'd tell him later.

Four more boxes and she'll be done. Not yet six o'clock and the sun is still hot, maybe a hundred degrees. For a moment she stops, listening to the breeze rustling the fronds of the date palms. She turns, looks for Mount Jacinto. Snow clings in improbable patches. Next spring, early, maybe she and Marina would take Carolina up there on the tram. Sometimes the sudden intensity of her love for all this, this desert mountain place, surprises her, catches in her throat.

She throws Marina's dresses over her arm and slides the box of Carolina's stuffed animals out from the back seat, starts to lock up Marina's car. But Leonard calls from the front porch saying he will back out and she can put both cars in the garage. She gets behind the wheel of the wagon. Leonard's instincts about this are good: the less visible they are the better. The garage door opens and Leonard's lemon meringue convert-

ible backs out. She pulls Marina's car in tight against the wall, then her own up alongside the washer and dryer. When she enters the house through the kitchen, the heavy garage door closes behind her, automatically.

"This feels like Fort Knox," says Yo, gratefully taking the gin and tonic Len holds out to her.

"It's pretty secure. There's a wall around the whole development and a guard at the gate. Well, you saw him when you came in, such as he is. Deputy Dawg, I call him. But these days any security is smoke and mirrors. Even Edith Ann here's an illusion."

Yo glances into the living room where Len's fawn-colored Great Dane lounges on the white carpet, licking its forearm thoughtfully. Carolina is making her way around the glass coffee table, clearing it of *Architectural Digests*. Marina sits with her drink, looking more relaxed than she has in two days.

"Harlow's the real watch dog," says Len, sitting down on the couch next to Marina. "Edith Ann is a total wimp. I tell myself if the chips were down she'd rouse herself up to kill on my behalf. But to be perfectly honest, I think she'd offer an intruder a vodka collins."

"Len," says Marina, "I feel perfectly safe."

"Well, there is a security system, but I used to trip the damn thing off taking a pee at night. Armed guards would pull up in front of the house. Lights everywhere. So embarrassing! I don't fool with it anymore. If you decide you want it, though, the instructions are in the bottom drawer of the kitchen desk.

"I think that's it. There's a note on the counter about the babies' food, and the vet, and where I'll be, just in case. Gil and Mac know the house and the babies, the routine. So call them if anything comes up."

"I think we're set," says Yo. "Thank you so much, dear."

Len gets to his feet. Marina and Yo give him parting hugs. The little dog dances around their feet, while Carolina grabs for her.

"This is good for me too, you know," says Len. "I don't have to worry about the girls. Any of them."

Yo pushes her cart of jiggling equipment down the hall of the third floor. Some kind of uproar is going on in the doorway of 314, where she is supposed to draw blood samples from a Mrs. Hartly. Grace Gutierrez is saying to a younger nurse, "Mrs. Reed is not supposed to be in here at all; Mrs. Reed has a private room," and the younger nurse is saying she's just following instructions.

Yo sticks her head in, saying, "Hartly? Bette Jo Hartly?" She stops dead, because she thinks she knows the woman in the near bed, the one whose body is a territory under dispute. And yet she looks like a lot of other middle-aged Palm Springs women: short curly blond hair, eyebrows plucked and shaped into a surprised arch, neck cords strung taut by the tensions of gracious living, an air of eager exhaustion. The same look she has seen replicated, satirized in the makeup of drag queens. Sometimes Gilberto looks like this.

"I know you from somewhere," she says to the woman.

"Biscuit Reed, Coachella Public Library. I got your books for you."

"Yes," says Yo, "I remember you. What're you in for?" She takes her hand. There is something about this woman and her wide open gaze that makes Yo want to do something for her. Maybe run down the hall with her to the elevator, get her out of here. She sees herself racing down Dinah Shore Drive pushing Biscuit Reed in her hospital bed, pursued by doctors, nurses, her dumb-ass husband.

"She doesn't belong here," says Grace, starting to roll the bed. "She's scheduled for a private room."

"I'm Harold Reed's wife," Biscuit explains. "They're going to fix my eyes tomorrow, from the blepharoplasty."

"Fix them?" says Yo, noticing now her lids and cheeks are bruised.

"Yes, just the tiniest little correction so I can close them at night. They're supposed to close. You know, when I sleep. Nothing major."

Grace and the other nurse nudge the bed around tables and chairs and ferry it out into the hall.

"Damn," says Yo, under her breath. "Damn."

"How's a person supposed to get any rest around here?" the woman in the remaining bed says. "All this commotion going on."

"Mrs. Hartly?"

"Call me BJ."

BJ has a round flat face, big woman. Probably headed for the body shop. Liposuction, she'd guess. While Yo wipes BJ's arm with alcohol, the woman's attention drifts back to the "Columbo" rerun playing up near the ceiling.

"I wouldn't mind a man like Columbo," she says. "Ever notice those eyes of his? Clean him up a little bit and you'd have a nice-looking man. Wife ought to be ashamed letting him run around looking like that."

Yo keeps working, is looking for the vein.

"I never can understand, though," she continues, "why they have to kill somebody in these shows. Every single time."

Yo laughs. "I guess there's got to be a murder or there wouldn't be a mystery to solve."

"So much violence in the world today," continues BJ, eyes closed in contemplation.

"Yes," Yo agrees, glancing at the supine form of Bette Jo Hartly, "all kinds." She unwraps the elastic tourniquet from her arm and begins labeling the vials.

"You know you just got to wonder," continues BJ. "I mean, what if they went ahead and had a mystery without any murder? I mean, why not? You'd still get Columbo and those big, brown eyes."

Yo pats her arm and heads down the hall.

May 26, 1983

1 ⌀ Aunt Josie's been wearing Gary Luna's house slippers again. When her husband visits her now it's mostly in the form he walked in when they met thirty years ago at the Indio Date Festival. Gary Luna was one of the Bird Song Dancers then, all dressed up in feathers, looking so proud. Now when he wants to come home for a while, she first hears the feathers, then feels his presence.

She hasn't seen him yet today; he missed the Perry Mason movie at eight, but he might watch "20/20" with her at ten. One of his favorite shows. Right now she's sitting in her La-Z-Boy running her fingers down stalks of dried desert lavender, harvesting the small buds onto the newspaper open in her lap. She went Wednesday morning early into Cahuilla Canyon for the lavender, some yucca for her shampoo, sage for headaches, mallow for tea. Maybe that's why Gary's been on her mind all day, all week. Cahuilla Canyon was where los viejos had done their harvesting. They had passed over, but left their messages behind them in the rocks: paintings, arrowheads, grinding holes.

She needs this lavender to make medicine for Jaime's hands, all broken out with sores from those chemicals at the golf course. Took no care of himself, since Sally left him. Working and seeing his son weekends was all that mattered to him anymore. And that fancy black truck of his. Well, one day he'd meet somebody nice he cared about, maybe get married. He could take his time, though. All this divorce business. People floating around like runaway balloons, everywhere she looked.

She breathes in the lavender. Umm. Glances at the clock. Twenty till ten. Weekends, if she's alone, she likes to have dinner late. Pull up the TV tray to the couch and eat a little something while she watches prime time. Perry Mason had kept her in her seat, but now she's hungry. She's had a pot of frijoles going on the stove since morning.

She funnels the lavender buds from the newspaper into the great blue bowl on the sewing machine, brings olive oil from the kitchen and pours in a cup or two, stirs it with a wooden spoon, covers it up with a *Life* magazine, and sets it to steep by the window.

She glances at the cover. Movie stars floating too. The whole world. And now it turned out that Marina and her baby were floating too, chased by a white man with fists too quick, somebody rich with bad ideas.

But they are safe for now, the three of them. Hidden even she didn't know where, and that's good. What one person knows pretty soon everybody's going to know. Not even Crescencio knows where they are.

He's over to Yolanda's place right now, keeping an eye on things. Everybody moving around, not sleeping in their own beds. Well it's like Gary Luna always said, one thing you can count on is you never know what's going to happen next. But it's going to happen. That's what the Cahuillas said. It meant you never did think you had it bad. You just had it, that was all.

She laughs, and goes into the kitchen, finds her good iron skillet and scrapes in a tablespoon of bacon fat—Yo would tell her use the canola oil—and heats it up. She likes the smell of fat. Then she ladles some beans into the pan and mashes them up good with the back of a wooden spoon. Grates up some of that nice Jack cheese from the A&P, stirring it into the beans. Then fresh raw garlic for the blood and to keep away colds. The beans are starting to stick to the pan when she remembers the tomatoes on her window ledge. Crescencio dropped them by this afternoon on his way to Yo's.

That Crescencio. If she didn't know better she might say he was in love with la señora. The heart was a funny thing. She rinses the tomato and slices through cleanly with her sharpest knife, studies the intricacies of the luminous film of green, seeds suspended in heart-shaped wedges on her open palm. On a white plate she arranges them, then thinks about tortillas. Fresh flour ones would be nice. She glances up at her yellow teapot clock on the wall. Four minutes till ten. No time. She puts two store-bought corn tortillas into the toaster oven and turns it on.

In the living room she sets up her TV tray, folds a paper napkin and places her fork on top. From the refrigerator she takes one of Jaimito's dark frosty bottles of Modelo and opens it up.

The tortilla oven clicks. Everything is ready now. She spoons up the beans alongside the tomatoes, grabs her plate, la mantequilla. The beer will not fit. She comes back for it, places it on the tray. Turns on the TV to warm it up. Has she got everything? Yes, just right. She adjusts the sound and slides in behind her table.

Tonight on "20/20" is Geraldo Rivera. She likes it that the reporter is going to be Mexican, like her. You don't see that too much. Gary Luna might feel like watching. She sips her beer.

This Geraldo starts talking about the AIDS so she listens up close, on account of Yolanda. And then he is talking about the blood supply. Just before he says it, she hears the rustle of feathers. And then the very same moment Gary Luna sits down beside her, Geraldo Rivera is telling the whole nation about how the blood supply has the AIDS virus in it. She will listen, get it all, then tell everybody. Everybody who would listen.

2 🖉 Ellen Ramos sits at the far end of her parents' living room folding clean laundry, looking up from time to time, watching her father and sister as they lean their heads in close together during commercials, talking about the Perry Mason movie she has been unable to keep her mind on.

Ellen arrived from Boston that morning, spent the day with her mother and Josefina while her father got in a game of golf. Or rather Josie had spent the day perched up on her mother's bed watching old colorized movies with the sick woman, giving her water, the only thing her mother could keep down, brushing her hair. Ellen had busied herself catching up on the household chores, until her sister arrived. She brought Josefina lunch on a tray.

All day long she swallowed her guilt. Guilt for not coming sooner, for not coming more often, staying longer, for not understanding just how ill her mother really had been. For preferring the convolutions of her own life in the east. For avoiding her father by abandoning her mother. Her mother, who had seemed always to be raising three children instead of two.

How he had devoured her time with his needs. How he had gulped up her culture because his was stronger, louder, more competitive, had more money, moved faster. Ellen had to learn Spanish in school as an adult because when she and her sister were children their father didn't know the language and didn't want to. Her mother's language had been concealed under this house, beneath his church, his business, his death culture, just as her name had been obliterated by his, until she, Ellen, had reclaimed it.

Her father's friends all dressed in parakeet clothes, read no books, had no thoughts, existed only to consume and to play golf. But the clincher had come this afternoon.

Weak as she was, her mother would not use the bedpan. Josie explained her mother would walk to the bathroom using her cane, that Ellen should stand nearby—just in case—but that her mother could do everything herself. The toil of it almost broke Ellen's heart: the slow, careful movement, the short distance stretching out before her mother like a lifetime. But when she approached the toilet, turned, lifted her gown, then Ellen saw it: a patchwork of stitches, ribbons of flesh crossing and recrossing, the whole re-creation of her stomach and thighs hanging loose like elephant flesh. That was when she had wanted to kill him, her father.

When he came home, she wanted to talk. He didn't. He wanted to watch the news, told her the surgeries had been her mother's idea, not his. But where had she gotten that idea, Ellen had demanded? She saw the fury in him rising, saw again in her mind his hand upraised against her.

Violence was everywhere, tattooed on the bodies of women. She would not harbor it inside herself, nor would she fill her mother's house with it in these last days. "All right," she had said. "It's all right."

She sets aside the laundry and moves quietly down the hall. Her mother has slipped into uneasy sleep again, her eyes half open, then closing, sometimes a murmured phrase. As Ellen stands there watching, she hears the doorbell, hears her father's voice rise in anger. She rushes to the door. There stands Josefina, and just behind her, the gardener, her brother Crescencio. They have something to tell la señora, something she would want to know. Something of mucha importancia. "Come in," says Ellen. "Please come in, both of you."

May 27, 1983

Ellen is not sure if her mother has understood. She is not sure the solving of the mystery last night occupies a significant position in her mother's personal narrative. If anything, her mother has slipped deeper into her own world of dream, murmurs bits of sentences, questions; calls out in her sleep.

Her father seems confused too. At breakfast Ellen tried to talk with him about AIDS, what this might mean. He showed her instead the tall bottle of clear liquid the doctor sent over. Morphine. Use this, he said.

Now he must go to work, though it is Saturday. He has important business there. In her mind, Ellen sees him crouched behind his desk, protecting himself like a small, fierce animal, teeth bared.

Left alone, the two sisters talk. Since Andrea is pregnant, they agree it would be best if she left. No one knows how people get AIDS. With the taxi waiting, she bends to kiss her mother's forehead. "Josefina," cries her mother in alarm.

"Hush, hush," Ellen tells her. "It's all right."

At lunchtime her father does not come home. Her mother

has begun an incessant moaning. The nurse returns her call. Reminds her about the morphine. Tells her not to worry about addiction. There's no point.

Ellen's ideas about death she is about to see refuted. She has always believed people deserved clarity as the end approached. By three in the afternoon she has read the label on the bottle and given her mother the correct dose. Her mother sleeps calmly now, breathes evenly for two or three hours. Wakes thirsty. Ellen drops water into her mouth through a straw.

Her mother asks where her red sweater is.

Ellen tells her it's safe in her drawer.

At eight the pain is back. Her father came home at seven, took a shower, and fell asleep in front of the television. Ellen looks at the bottle. Measures the next dose carefully. Thinks she sees Crescencio outlined against the date palm.

At ten her mother wakes again. It's early for the next dose. Ellen feels the pain herself, a kind of rawness in every cell. A cellular desperation. She gives her water, drop by drop. As much as she will take. By now, nothing is coming out. Whatever is in her body will stay there, all fluids trapped, dammed up. Her mother moans.

Ellen gives her the next dose early. She may have poured out a little too much this time. Not a lot. Just a little. Eliana says, "That's better." And sleeps.

But the time between doses keeps diminishing, as if time is compacting, becoming a distillation. It's almost five in the morning before Ellen finally understands. Understands why the doctor sent over the morphine and did not talk to them. Understands why she has been left alone with this enormous bottle of liquid and her mother's pain.

Ellen is very clear. She knows exactly what to do.

May 28, 1983

1 ✑ The light has left the world. George Townsend sits in the chair next to his wife, but she no longer breathes for him. His daughter is making all the necessary calls, is making the arrangements, but in the meantime he will sit here beside her, waiting. Morning light is streaming in through the sliding door, forming a bright wedge on the foot of her bed.

For the first time George Townsend adjusts his head at an angle to see what it is his wife has been looking at as she lay in her bed all these days. Years. The triangle of petunias, strands of a flaming bougainvillea climbing a trellis, a grapefruit tree with white painted trunk, a date palm, the mountain beyond. And as he looks, the gardener of all this appears before his eyes. Crescencio stands, peering in through the glass door at Eliana, his hand held up against the reflection.

Then he is gone, and in a moment the doorbell rings. "No, no, by God, no," George hears himself shout. Strange, the familiarity of his own voice reverberating throughout the house. He looks over at his wife. He quiets himself, for her sake, and he waits.

His daughter appears in the doorway. "Papa," she says, "they'd like to come in for a minute. Josefina and Crescencio."

He hears Crescencio saying, "I just want to look at her," but he seems not to be saying it to anyone in particular. Then he and Josie are both in the room, standing silently side by side, respectful, his own daughter tall behind them. As if they are posed for a family portrait.

His own daughter has left him to join them—he knows this—the daughter who accuses, demands, complains. The one who only yesterday said to him, "Ellie, Ellie, Ellie! Just once why couldn't you call her Eliana! Her name is Eliana!"

He looks at her now, his daughter, standing with them, the three of them looking together at the still figure on the bed. He wants to protest, explain, "But that was her love name." He opens his mouth to speak it, but the three of them disperse in that moment as if the photograph is completed; they disappear, through the house, out the door, out of his life.

He turns to his wife. "Ellie?" he says softly. "Eliana?"

2 ✐ David has been hungry for the last hundred miles, but he doesn't want to stop. His eye keeps straying toward the billboards, as he drives through Beaumont, then Banning, looking for a decent place to eat. It's past two and he hasn't had lunch, keeps looking but for some reason he decides each time against stopping. Twice he started to pull over, then swerved back onto the highway. His hands just

keep gripping the steering wheel of his gray rental car. He has been waiting four months for this. Too long.

Like a man doing time. Tried and found guilty by Isabel Ochoa Dryfus: witness, prosecutor, and judge. When all he had ever wanted to do was provide for her. Love her. Care for her.

He's going to find her now. Has the address. Her phone number. He's going to find her and let her know what his love is really like. He knows she loves him, needs him. And suddenly he remembers—as if he is there—Isabel's mother in the living room in Juárez bringing her husband a drink; she is wearing a flowing hostess dress in rich broad stripes that sways as she moves, and the way she hands him the drink, seeks out his gaze, it seems as if they are alone together in the room. This is what David wants, has wanted ever since that evening. He wants a home like the one Isabel came from. That's all he's ever wanted.

David knows he'll have to be understanding with her. Isabel probably never really recovered from the death of her mother. She's not stable. He'll go slow, treat her now like a flower. Like the flower she is.

But as he thinks this, makes this resolve, the car pulls hard and sudden to the left and he hears the unmistakable thwap, thwap, thwap of the left front tire blown. He fights the wheel, gradually pulls the shuddering car over to the right-hand shoulder. Gets out into terrible heat.

A hot breeze lifts his tie and flings it over his shoulder. His hair blows back in the blast. No one stops. A train rages past, sounding its horn into the vacant landscape. David stands at the side of the highway, staring ahead at the San Gorgonio pass, gazing helplessly at bleak hills studded with white windmills whirling their indifferent, crazy arms. Thousands and thousands of them.

He locks the car and begins walking toward Palm Springs.

May 29, 1983

1 ✍ "Well, I got to hand it to you," says Silvia Cedeño when Yo walks into the lab early Monday morning. "Matter of fact I tried to call you Saturday, but nobody answered."

"I'm staying with friends for a while. Hand what to me?"

"You were one hundred percent right about the blood supply, and Geraldo Rivera said so to millions of people Friday night on '20/20.' It was even in the Sunday papers. You didn't see it? I know your friend Harold Reed saw it, and he's rushing around trying to cover his sweet ass.

"Some people are saying Geraldo's wrong, and some people are saying the report's exaggerated, and some people are saying well we knew that for years. But the fact is, everybody's got something to say and now they're saying it.

"Remember that day you were telling me about Anabelle What's-her-name? That she really discovered those belts up there in the sky and not that famous scientist at all? This is the exact same thing. From now on when people say it was Geraldo Rivera first said the blood supply was not safe, know what I'm going to say? No way; it was Yolanda Ramírez. That's who."

2 ⌬ Marina pulls the red Camaro into Ralph's parking lot, wonders if it would be best to park up close and get into the store quickly, or far away to be less conspicuous. Red's conspicuous anyway; she would never have a red car herself, had sat in the Earl Sheib paint shop in Los Angeles deliberating forever over the color to paint the station wagon she had taken from David's driveway that morning almost four months ago. Finally she had decided on blue to calm her nerves, and now here she is in vibrant red, remembering the shame she felt in Salvador Greenfeather's office only minutes before, when he had said to her that unspeakable thing.

Buying the groceries would help settle her before she goes home to Yolanda. Home. A concept that's become like a funhouse mirror with alternatives leading off infinitely (Juárez, Des Moines, Coachella, Palm Springs, Tucson). Her name the same (Isabel Ochoa, Isabel Dryfus, Marina Lomas). Marina, the name Yo prefers because she knows her by it, because—she says—Marina chose it.

The car is heating up inside. But she must look carefully in all directions before getting out. Yet she does not know exactly what she is looking for. A rented car. A face, handsome, fair, controlled. That knows its name. That will never be questioned. A face that looks always as if it belongs, wherever it is.

"Me llamo," she says, then steps out into the heat, locks the door, walks quickly toward the broad window blaring specials. Tall block letters saying in red, double coupons.

Doors wheeze open admitting her into bone-rattling cold. Muzak. People dreaming down aisles of food.

She can never quite get used to American supermarkets, always forgets what she came for. Takes refuge—as she does now—in the produce section. She holds a plum. Caresses the greens of carrots. Seeks aroma in the tomatoes. Holds a purple onion. Puts an eggplant into her basket. Two zucchinis. She buys corn in fragrant husks. She smells Mexico in the tassels. Misses her father, the ghost of her mother. Holds the flesh of a mango as if it were a hand.

3 ✎ Damn! It's six o'clock and Marina is not back from the lawyer's yet. Carolina is rhythmically smacking Leonard's sculpted glass coffee table with a wooden mallet. Maybe Yo should go ahead and feed her. Edith Ann is lying under the grand piano trying to Zen out but no use. Yo, who only two or three months ago thought of herself as traveling light, now has a lover, a baby, a house, a Great Dane, a poodle, and a husband-in-law tracking them all down. Eventually she will have to give the house and dogs back, but what about Marina and Carolina? And what about the husband?

More than once Yo has caught herself looking out the windows, studying angles of the yard through Len's many mirrors, jumping at moving light refracted from cars. And Harlow has a way of running to the front door and barking like crazy. Then when Yo leaps up and looks through the peephole, Harlow strolls away looking bored. Little dogs. Damn.

She would get herself a beer, assemble Carolina's dinner, feed the dogs. Marina should be back soon. Her appointment with Salvador was at four. How long could it take? She flips the cap off a Corona and squeezes a wedge of lime down into it, takes some carrots out of the refrigerator. Leonard is so clean. She should talk to him, really, about AIDS. Make sure he understands about being careful. Ribbons of carrot tumble into the sink. Carolina loves carrot sticks, celery—anything she can eat with her hands.

AIDS. She thinks of Silvia telling her she was right about the blood, like that was going to make her feel good. Well, in a way it had. She took a low-down kind of mean pleasure in being one up on Harold Reed. Now the hospital would start doing something. Would have to. All of them. That did make her feel good.

But the problem was not about to go away because of one TV show. What remained was the fact of AIDS. What remained was Gilberto turning into a calavera right before her eyes. What remained was Eliana Townsend's death on Sunday and her father in pain that he didn't know how to talk about.

Funeral Wednesday, and she would have to go. For her father. She remembered seeing Eliana Townsend only once, when Yo and her father stopped in the truck to unload a couple of bougainvilleas and a rubber tree. To tell the truth, Yo had been prepared to dislike her. Thought she was some kind of closet pocha.

But when Eliana had come out onto the patio that afternoon wiping her hands on a dish towel, smiling in pleasure at the new plants, at meeting Crescencio's daughter, there had been something in that moment Yo was not going to forget.

Thoughts, connections now scatter as Yo hears the sound of Leonard's books hitting the floor. Carolina. Then Harlow starts to yap, and when Edith Ann bestirs herself, giving deep, echoing barks, Yo knows for sure that Marina is home.

She hears the garage door opening, and then the car door. Yo stands waiting, holding back Carolina from a tumble. "Need help?"

"No, I've got it Yo, just two bags."

She comes in smelling of eggplant and lemons and corn. Yo takes the bags, kisses her. "I got Carolina's dinner ready. Working on the dogs. How'd it go with Sal?"

Marina goes pale.

"Bad news?" asks Yo.

"He made me mad, querida. Estoy muy enojada." She picks up Carolina, nuzzles her, murmurs in Spanish, sets her into her chair, puts her thick plastic dish on the table and scoots her in, sits down beside her.

Yo places the bags on the counter. Sits opposite. Both dogs are staring at her. "Oh all right." She gets up and fills their dishes with food, big chunks for Edith Ann, tiny kibble for Harlow. She sits back down to the sound of crunching in two keys. "Marina, what did he say?"

"He said, 'What a waste.' That's what he said."

"What's a waste?"

Carolina is smacking her dish with a raw carrot.

"Me with you."

"Bastard, I told you he had ideas," says Yo.

Marina shoots a warning glance at Yo. "I can't talk about it now."

Yo gets up, paces, looks out the window. "I hate this. What did he say about the other. Los negocios?"

Carolina picks up a pea carefully, turns, and drops it onto the floor. The poodle pounces.

"Doesn't look good," says Marina. "Maybe a fifty-fifty chance. We'll talk later." She cuts her eyes over to Carolina.

"I've never liked Salvador much, but damn I would have expected better than this."

"Es hombre."

Yo pours an icy Corona into one of Leonard's beautiful hand-blown goblets and sets it in front of Marina. "That doesn't explain his behavior. Much less excuse it."

Marina nods, tries relaxing into her chair. Yo wraps her arms around her, kisses her plum-colored hair, says, "Isabel, mi Isabel, is, is, is, Isabel."

4 ⬦ Crescencio stands with the green hose in his hand, water running into his daughter's plants. She's got a million things growing in pots and nothing planted in the ground. Everything temporary, like she could pack them all into the trailer, throw the hose in behind them, and be gone in half an hour. He'd really like to see her put something into the ground for a change. But maybe she's the one who's right. What's the good of it after all?

He and Josie had left Guerrero in the middle of the night, crossing the border inside a truck with no air, a night with no water, no food, no way to relieve themselves, lying there, lost, in the dark belly of a truck with people they didn't know, waiting for a man of no principles, un coyote. Un ladrón. Two hundred dollars he had taken from them; nearly everything they had.

At least Yolanda had it better. He moves the hose to the olive barrel with the small lemon tree. She needs to feed it. Maybe he would do that tomorrow. All this strangeness. Yolanda and Marina hiding out with the baby, just like they were wanted. Like criminals. And the man who chases them is somehow the one with all the right on his side. The man wearing a suit.

Josie was right. He was getting damn tired of these suit men deciding how things were going to be. He had not been surprised when Townsend had fired him. "Let you go," is how ese hombre had said it when he showed up for work this morning, same as all the other mornings. Pushed fifty dollars into his hand and then let him go.

"Well, gabacho, I let you go too," he says to the lemon tree. He turns off the water, coils up the hose. Yolanda needs a small garden, that's for sure. Lechuga, some tomatoes maybe.

He can't decide whether he should stay here tonight or go on to his own house. It doesn't seem to make a difference somehow. How do you keep an eye on somebody's place? How could you take care of anything or anybody in this kind of world? Well, he would go inside and see did she have a beer. Decide later.

Hot inside. Must have set that thermostat too high yesterday, trying to save a little on Yo's utilities. He lowers it; the swamp cooler starts to throb, the sound of water trickling down. Crescencio steps on a duck that squeals. La niña. Signs of her all over the place. Almost like they was a family, like the baby was Yo's too. He finds a Corona in the refrigerator—only two left—searches in the drawer for the opener, sits down at the kitchen table. Magazines all over the table and a teething biscuit stuck to the cover of one called *Ms.* They had left in a big hurry, those two, and the little baby.

And now he is here to keep an eye on things. The other place too, both of them. He carries two keys in the pocket of his work pants. He glances down the hill at the turquoise trailer that is Marina's and the beaten-down grass where the clothesline is strung up. Two little windows spaced out like eyes looking back.

He thinks about the "Rockford Files" and Jim Rockford living in a beat-up trailer that looks a lot like Marina's. He thinks about Jim Rockford's father always sitting at the table having a beer whenever his son comes home from a big case, just like Crescencio is doing now. ¿Cómo se llama? Rocky, he is called, the father. Rocky, he's always hanging around just keeping an eye on things. Like Crescencio's doing now.

The beer is beginning to settle him down. He feels better. At first he didn't know what to do with his lady gone out of the world. Seemed at first like something had been sucked out of his belly, like when he takes the elevator down from the top floor of the bank building. Vacuumed out of him. Like the liposuction, quizás. Maybe Eliana had felt like this right after her operation. Emptied out, confused. Death had rushed into all her empty spaces.

Somehow this beer is turning into tears. He swallows them down, remembers the daughter, Ellen. The daughter looking just like her mother. Beautiful, like her. Ellen. Eliana. Named for her; living after her. Ellen Ramos.

He has his Yolanda. But she is not going to have any kids, she always tells him. Sometimes she says, Things stop here, old man. Crescencio thinks he will have that last beer, check Marina's place out, and then maybe go on home. On top of the refrigerator he sees a pair of field glasses. Yolanda likes to walk into the canyons and look at the birds. Sometimes up high she sees those old shaggy mountain sheep with the curvy horns, the ones almost gone. Extinct, Yo says.

Like him.

He opens the beer and sits down with the binoculars. Light is beginning to soften around him. He takes an apple from the abandoned basket of fruit on the table and bites in. The green tartness feels like something he somehow needs. He aims the glasses out the window and sweeps the open spaces between the trailers, runs them across and into the brown Indio Hills. He is Rocky Rockford, keeping an eye on things. Rocky, and he sees something now.

A car. A car where there had not been one. Silver. The color of fog. Parked a ways off from Marina's clothesline. He trains the binoculars on the turquoise trailer. A man comes into view like he is backing away from the front door. A man in brown slacks and a tie. White man. White shirt. Tall. Then he walks all the way around the trailer, keeps looking in windows, like he doesn't belong there, yet somehow has a right.

When the man pulls away in his silver car Crescencio grabs the apple, locks up quick, and gets in his truck. Now it seems like he is not Rockford's father but becoming Rockford himself, the one who follows people, doesn't just sit in the trailer waiting. Now he's more important.

But he knows not to follow too close. He gets up on the freeway, driving way back, slumped low behind the wheel. Crescencio understands this kind of man's not going to see him anyway. A gardener, Mexican, invisible, nadie.

They get off together at the Gene Autry exit, head south toward Palm Springs. Finally the silver car turns down Calle Ocotillo and parks in front of the Casa Diva Guest House, the very place where Yo told him to go if he ever noticed anything funny.

Things are falling into place, like they do for Rockford near the end of the show. Yo said the time would come.

He pulls past the gray car and parks quick in a spot on the opposite side of the road, shuts down the truck. Jim Rockford always sits in his car and waits. Maybe gets some coffee in a paper cup, if there's someplace close. Jelly doughnut. Crescencio looks down the street, up the street, nothing but small motels and guest houses behind hedges of oleander for as far as he can see. He cranks down the window and re-laxes a little into the lumpy front seat. Thinks about eating the apple but it's turned a little brown in the heat. He's not hungry anyway. He'll get something later.

He'll need to talk to the man named Mac, hombre with the red hair, ask him to call Yolanda and tell her about ese gabacho. Make a report. Crescencio himself doesn't know where Yolanda is. That's part of the plan. Secrets can only be kept if nobody knows them.

In a little while the man comes out. Crescencio steals a peek in the rearview mirror. He can see by the pink light of sunset. The man is about thirty-five, maybe more. His suit says money. Kind of rosy-brown. He's standing there next to the man that must be Mac, red hair, skinny, like Yo said. He's shaking his head like he don't know nothing. Then suit man takes out a little white card and writes on it fast, hands it to the skinny man. They shake hands, and suit man goes back to his silver car. Then the silver car lights up and moves slowly toward Crescencio, passes him like he is not there, quiet, like a ghost ship. Everything is on purpose with this man. But he doesn't know everything.

Crescencio waits until he is out of sight, gets out of the truck, and walks toward the gate that leads to the man with the red hair.

June 1, 1983

1 ⚲ Yo steers the lady car carefully into the church lot and parks. Her father sits next to her in his suit, brown with pinstripes, that he has not worn since her mother died five years ago. His eyes are deep and she can see the pain seeping and pooling inside them.

She looks out onto the lawn where people are collecting. She can see Harold Reed, Meredith Disenhouse, a couple of the body shop boys. Their wives. Yo is not in the mood to hear fine sentiments. She doesn't even want to say hello to anybody. She glances in the rearview mirror and sees her aunt's round face beneath her black straw hat, her shoulders against white leather.

Yo swings open the heavy door, tries to adjust her merciless undergarments as she makes her way around the back of the Lincoln. She is wearing her dress for her father, along with all its requisite backup gear. The crotch of her panty hose has already begun stealing toward her knees. She opens the back door for Tía Josie, who is wearing a black dress covered in little white polka dots and her brooch with the palm tree inside. Jaime gets out of the back and opens the front door for Crescencio. Brother and sister link arms and make their way toward the church. Yo and her cousin fall in behind. Tía Josie keeps patting Crescencio's arm, giving him little squeezes.

Inside Yo sees her father look around for the holy water and then realize he is not in a Catholic church. Yo finds she is wondering which side of the church they should sit on, because she tends to confuse weddings and funerals. Owning only one dress reinforces this ambiguity. Then her eye falls on the casket.

The casket is standing open. Eliana looks like a passenger in some kind of space-age mass transit system. She is riding a little too high in her capsule, has been made up within an inch of her life. This is not the woman Yo met that day, the handsome and gracious woman bending to smell the bougainvillea.

Aunt Josie reaches across Crescencio and squeezes Yo's arm. Suddenly Yo remembers Eliana from another time. Her mother's funeral had just ended and she was standing on the church steps with her father. Eliana stepped forward, touched her arm in a way that released like a spring all the longing Yo had ever had for her own mother and the simple gift of her approval. This phantom feeling that she had never at the time examined now comes flooding back, dragging with it all the mother-loss Yo has ever known.

She fights back tears, vows not to forget that moment, the woman. Her father sits next to her with his hands clasped and his lips moving. She wishes she could call up for him the old comfort of Latin, candles, incense, and the soothing sounds of women telling their beads. Aunt Josie has a firm grip on his arm, anchoring him to this world.

Yo looks back at the figure in the coffin, calms herself by focusing on this moment, this face. And as she concentrates on what is material here, this costuming, she becomes aware of something strangely familiar. She has seen this face before. But where?

And then it comes to her. Eliana's death mask is twin to the face from the library, the trusting face in the hospital, the face of Biscuit Reed.

⁓

Back at her father's house Yo checks him in the rearview mirror the instant before he gets out of the back seat. Worse, this time. A deeper thing. He leans in the window. She asks him, "You going to be all right?"

"Oh yeah."

"Remember, you're not going to check my house anymore. You're off duty. Not Marina's either. Too dangerous. ¿Me entiendes? Ese vato es un loco."

"Yes, he's very bad," says Crescencio shaking his head. "I don't know how a man gets like that. You got a right to your own home, mi'ja."

"You stay en casa tonight, rest up. Okay? Don't go nowhere."

"Okay," he says.

Jaime kisses him, claps his shoulders twice, and says, "Take care, Tío. Call me you need anything. Hear?"

Crescencio nods, makes a waving gesture like it's time for them all to leave him to his own thoughts, in his own house. Yolanda watches him make his way slowly up the front steps, open the door, and disappear inside. Tía Josie places her hand on Yo's arm. "He's going to be all right, Yolanda. He's strong. It's just going to take a little time."

Yo starts the car, turns it around, and heads back the way they came. In her mirror she can see through billowing dust her cousin Jaime following in his black pickup.

"You're probably going to hear him start talking again about going back."

"Guerrero you mean? To Old Guerrero?"

"There ain't but one Guerrero for that one. Me, I'm at home right where I am. I'm a retired American citizen with a house, a car, and a TV with electricity to run it. Oh, I ain't saying I don't miss Guerrero. It sure was a pretty town. But I ain't no scuba diver, that's for sure." She laughs.

"Tía, I been thinking. If I was to leave here, if Marina and I have to go someplace else with the baby, could you and Papa get along okay, at least for a while?" She watches Jaimito in the rearview mirror, turning onto Palm Canyon, headed for the golf course.

"Thinking of leaving la Coachella?"

"Well we're okay for now, but pretty soon we've either got to go home or move on. We're both getting pretty jumpy right now. Can't take too much more of this. Marina keeps thinking she's being followed, and I got to admit ever since Papa saw that car around Marina's place I been staring into my rearview mirror. It's damn hard to think what to do."

"You girls can come stay with me in my house. I got plenty of room."

Yo pulls up under the cottonwoods in front of her aunt's house. "Right now we got to be careful about this man. He's mean and he's plenty mad. So you be careful too. Lock your house up good day and night, call Jaimito you see anything funny."

Aunt Josie gives her a kiss, opens the passenger door, then whispers quickly, "Don't worry, mi'ja, I'm not going to blow your cover," then hurries inside.

2 ✐ In that ambiguous zone between afternoon and evening, two women are swimming. There is no particular pattern. Sometimes they reach opposite ends of the pool at the same moment; other times they swim together, as if synchronized. Mostly they simply swim, water running in currents off their moving bodies. They are swimming themselves clean.

One has just come from a funeral and one has just visited her lawyer. Which amounts to the same thing.

Inside the house a baby stands in her crib, quietly handling three suspended objects meant to soothe her into the night's sleep: a dog, a dish, a spoon. Outside her open window, too high for her to see, her mothers are swimming themselves clean.

But this is not their house. This house belongs to a friend vacationing in Aspen. This house is inside a walled community with a guard at the gate. The guard is watching "Celebrity Golf" on a small screen and taking an occasional nip from the half pint of Jim Beam he always keeps in his jacket pocket for emergencies.

In the master bedroom there is a California king-size bed where the women have carelessly cast their clothes. The friend's poodle is curled up neatly on a pair of panty hose. The other dog, a Great Dane, lies over an air conditioning vent in the living room, sleeping noisily, all four feet from time to time twitching almost imperceptibly, an ear cocking in the direction of a phantom intruder.

Outside could be a river. So much water moving. Women in the water. Mermaids, even.

The woman who came from the funeral swims wearing only goggles, notices the light at the opposite end snap on by itself, watches the bubbles streaming from the kicking feet of her partner, marks the patterns of shadows on the pool wall, how their arms, their legs could be just one creature swimming.

The other woman wears nothing. Moves easily. Feels her blood moving, cleaning itself. She is a fish moving freely.

3 ⌀ In the late afternoon when Crescencio pulls into his daughter's trailer park he gets a funny feeling in his belly. Yo told him not to come, to stay away from the man in the silver car. But es verdad, he couldn't spend one more minute stretched out on that old couch in his empty house wearing his brown suit, the one he buries his women in.

He's a man used to doing. When shadows lengthened he was used to driving by la señora's house to see was the light on next to her bed, was the curtain pulled tight or maybe could she see by the garden lights the flowers he kept planted near her door. Wasn't going to go there anymore not ever.

Knew where he was going to go instead when he changed out of his brown suit and into his work pants, knew when his fingers closed around those two loose keys left in his pocket from day before yesterday, the keys given to him by his daughter so he could keep an eye on things.

He pulls slow past Yo's trailer and then swings down to Marina's place. Nobody there, but he keeps on going without knowing why, parks down by that empty trailer Simón has let fall to pieces. He turns off the engine and sets the hand brake.

He keeps forgetting to take food. In the morning had been the funeral. No use putting meals on top of grief. After that, all day he had spent inside his house, lying there in that brown suit like a dead man laid out, blinds closed to keep out the worst of the sun, and besides it felt better to be in the dark. On such a day.

When the woman goes out of his life, a man stops eating. The woman marks his time, shapes his days by her cycling, her cooking, flowers on the table in a blue vase. When she leaves, he eats his own bile, or Burger King. And the man exists to protect her, protect the house that she makes beautiful.

All day long Crescencio has been thinking about the women slipping out of his grasp, women walking in danger that he doesn't know how to hold off. The world made a dark turn at some point.

The men in suits had unleashed the waters of the earth on Guerrero. Only Julia Zamora in her little boat could guard it now, she who believes the waters will one day recede, the town emerge, shining in the sun.

You got to live in this world, Crescencio, his wife had said. But what did that mean? What does it mean now? He had heard Mr. Townsend say many times the world was going to hell in a handbasket. Maybe Mr. Townsend felt the same as him, like he didn't know how to keep the women safe anymore.

He sees Mr. Townsend sitting in his dark kitchen in Palm Springs and he sees Julia Zamora fishing over the baseball diamond in Guerrero and he knows that his daughter cannot return to her own house bought and paid for. He doesn't know how all these things have come to pass. And now sitting in his truck in a trailer park in Coachella he knows there is something he, Crescencio Ramírez, must do.

But what is it?

As he sits thinking these thoughts he feels the seat next to him take on the shape of someone he knows, a slight complaint maybe from the old springs accepting weight, a certain warmth filling the cab. Must be Gary Luna's here.

Gary Luna tells him to take his gun from under the seat. Crescencio leans down and eases it out, wrapped like always in a dirty rag. But the gun itself is clean. Loaded. Like always. Cared for, like his tools. He unwraps it carefully, gets out of the truck, leans for support as he struggles to place the gun somewhere. Pocket's too tight. Finally he wedges it into the waistband of his pants like he's seen Rockford do, gives it a pat, starts up the road. Like a man on an errand.

It's getting dark fast now, the sun has slipped behind the mountain, sudden, as it does. No moon yet. The air cooling. His feet know the way. He sees no one. In a little while he turns down the curving pathway to Marina's place. His hand finds the worn key in his pocket, the key with the rounded head. It feels warm in his hand from the heat of his body. The gun too is beginning to warm from the heat of his belly. He turns the key in the lock and goes inside.

The scent of babies caught inside the closed-up air of the trailer. Hot inside. In the glow from the clown night-light he can see a little. Outlines. Not much furniture. He starts to heave himself onto an old couch, feels the gun crowding him, sets it on the adjoining cushion. Like a companion.

What's he doing sitting next to a gun? What has brought him here, to this moment? Suddenly he feels the weight of the day, of all the days, like he could sink on through that couch, fall through the floorboards of the trailer, travel down through warm sand like one of those fringed-toed lizards he's seen over at the preserve, not stopping till he arrived at the core of this tired-out earth. He sits and breathes, just waiting for Gary Luna to take charge again. After he rests.

In a minute, though, his left hand skirts the gun, goes off exploring, falls into a hole like a mouse nest. Stuffing coming out. They don't have much, these people. His right hand finds Carolina's wind-up pillow, a magazine, then a pen stuck between the cushions. He knows by the feel of it that it's Yo's special green ink pen, thick and heavy, the one she paid so much money for so she could think better, she told him. He holds it in his rough hand, feeling the difference between his daughter and himself.

His daughter. This home and these people are part of her life. He glances over to the breakfast nook. He might have had a place at that table. Time to pay attention to the life close around you, something tells him. Somebody. Like a voice he can hear.

He gets up and leans in close to the window next to the table. A slim moon has worked its way loose and floats like a fishhook giving off just a little light now. He sees a man on foot, same as him. Suit man moving like a dark shadow toward his daughter's Airstream, then stopping. Trying the locked back door, then the kitchen window. In a minute he disappears around the front.

Crescencio sits down at the table to watch. He slips the green pen into his pocket. Pretty soon the shadow returns to the back door, tries it again like someone might have unlocked it in the meantime. Then the shape moves back to the kitchen window. Runs his hand along the edge, like he's looking for something. Everything real quiet with this one. And yet like he has a right to be here, to do this. To do anything.

Crescencio is going to have to move silently and without hesitation, so he stands slowly, waits for his body to unfold, listens to the little complaints of muscle and bone, then stills them. He picks up the heavy gun again, stuffs it back into his pants, more easily this time, knowing how.

Like coyote he slips stealthily out the back door and around the side, waits like the other in the shadows. Neither of them breathes. Two men in the night. Crescencio will have to move first, get closer. He is going to have to match the silence in the other. He is going to have to match his feeling of right.

His feet feel solid as he moves up the slope past Marina's clothesline, but something inside him floats. He moves with no sound, like the river beneath the streets. He pauses now beside an ocotillo that stands in the dark almost like a third man, and then he hears in the hush el otro, the stranger, moving again like it's his turn, a shadow slipping toward the bedroom window. The bedroom of his daughter.

Crescencio is close enough now. Close enough to hear the snap of the flimsy, rusted latches. Shadow man lifts out the screen and props it deliberately against the side of the trailer as if he is simply maintaining what he already owns. El patrón. But when he throws a leg over the ledge and begins hoisting himself up, he crosses a boundary, una frontera of much significance, this stranger, this man who wants to take away Marina and Carolina, his daughter's family. His own family.

Crescencio pulls the gun out and aims it like an accusing finger, trembling for a moment, then steadied by his strong left hand. Carefully he sights down the barrel like it is the long telescope of his life. Just for a moment he stands waiting, listening through the clear air—an owl answering an owl, the bark of a kit fox, the song of the crickets underlying everything, all this—then he pulls the trigger.